Chapter One

"Look, Tiffany, we just don't fit. I'm not sure how many more ways I can explain it to you," Thomas informs the female he's with as they're walking through the door. "As promised, you can still be a guest at the party. Maybe you will meet someone else tonight." In truth, he did not intend to escort her to the party. He only made his way back to the house to retrieve what he forgot.

"You're such an asshole, Thomas! Maybe I'll find your friend and hook up with him," Tiffany threatens with a glare.

Thomas flicks his hand dismissively while eyeing the couple on the couch. "Have at it," is spoken without care. He can't wait until the end of the school year which is only two weeks away. This fraternity isn't much of a brotherhood. Too much backstabbing and the brothers have no regard for treating women respectfully.

His dismissive treatment toward Tiffany, whom he just broke up with, isn't the best example. It's midnight and he doesn't have patience for her any longer. He had caught her cheating on him with another guy in his fraternity. The scene he walked into with her and the other guy could never be described by him as respectful. Tiffany desired to be fucked in the ass as rough as possible. To each their own in regards to a fetish, but that is a pleasure he could never bring himself to provide.

It's amazing how much an incident can change your perspective. Her once beautifully brown eyes turned plain and boring. Her soft black hair now feels like a dried-out cactus. The taste of her used to be something he craved, but now it feels like acid on his tongue. In truth, nothing changed except his desire for her. Why did he ever give her a chance in the first place?

The furniture downstairs was once new and attractive. As the school year progressed, the couches became quickly worn down by frequent activity. Thomas refuses to sit on the various stains embedded into the cushions. The shelves and counters are worn down by people sitting on them instead of the available seating. The table on which they're supposed to eat on has seen better days. Even if he hadn't heard the lewd stories of amorous activities done on the table, the evidence is there for anyone who wishes to look closely enough.

Once he realized the integrity of the fraternity or lack thereof, it was too late to find any other student housing in his budget. This fraternity is not a place he calls home. This is not a place he could ever entertain a guest or even show it off with pride. This is a dark secret he keeps from everyone, including his parents. They would of course find him a new place they couldn't afford just to make him happy. Depending on them to help with school already cost his pride a significant ding. His parents aren't poor, but they don't have the income it would take to pay a mortgage, rent for an apartment, along with the cost of schooling his scholarships didn't cover. Two more weeks, and he'll know better for the fall semester.

Since he walked through the door, he's been unable to take his eyes away from the petite female who's sitting on the puke green-colored couch covered with numerous stains. There's something familiar about her. Thomas can't quite see her face since it's hidden by her long blonde hair and the hands of one of his shady fraternity brothers. It doesn't help that the room is too crowded with dumb kids drinking their future away.

"Hey, Thomas, that chick on the couch was asking for you earlier. Seems Nate has her handled though," the young man whispers as he leans toward Thomas.

"Jack, did she say why she was asking for me? Or what her name is?" Thomas inquires as he tries his best to catch a glimpse of her face.

"She said she knows you. I think she just wanted access to the party. I wonder how much longer it'll take before Nate pulls her onto his lap and has his way with her. You know how much of a sucker he is for a short skirt. Such easy access to slide inside of her," Jack boasts with a slight hint of jealousy.

Thomas takes his eyes away from the couple long enough to glare fiercely at Jack for his lewd comment. To say it loud enough for people several feet away to hear if they cared enough to pay attention is another example of how little they respect the women they bed.

"I don't know why we accepted your pledge. You don't belong in this house," Jack says in response to the look Thomas gave.

"Don't expect me to return to this shit fest next year," Thomas seethes as Jack begins to walk away. Turning his eyes just in time to see the girl trying to bat at Nate's hands as he attempts to pull her onto his lap. It's not surprising that Nate doesn't take her resistance as a no. Time to go intervene.

There are not enough words in the English dictionary to express how much he detests this place. Walking closer toward the couch, her physique is becoming increasingly familiar. He can't place her just yet. Her long blonde hair is covering the side of her face and now she is facing away from him. His frustration keeps building at the fact that he still can't figure it out.

Nate won with his strength and currently has the mysterious female straddled over his lap with her hands pinned to her side. "She doesn't seem too willing to be on your lap, Nate," Thomas asserts with an air of irritation.

"The new ones never know how fun the ride is until they're on it, Thomas," Nate explains with arrogance.

At the mention of his name, the female whips her head around. "Thomas! I've been asking him where you were," the female slurs as she attempts to stand up.

"Savannah? What are you doing here?" Thomas hisses with anger.

Stumbling in reaction to his words, Nate takes the opportunity to pull her back onto his lap. This time her back is to his front and her skirt is splayed to reveal her barely concealing red underwear. He takes advantage of the situation by cupping over her underwear and holding her firmly in place by her crotch. "Holy shit, you're burning up," he shudders in excitement.

"Let her go," Thomas seethes as Savannah tries to pry Nate's hand off of her. He cannot hit Nate without hurting Savannah in the process.

"Wait your turn!" Nate bites back.

As they begin to argue, Savannah goes limp. "How much did you give her?" Thomas demands. He knows all too well about the ways they coax women into doing their bidding. Not long after his pledge was accepted, they pulled him off to the side to let him in on the trick for success. The anonymous call he made to the dean's office was unsuccessful.

Nate tosses Savannah's limp body off to the side then stands up to face Thomas. "Look, farm boy, I've tolerated you long enough. Now you're getting in the way of my count and that's unacceptable. Go hide in your room like you've done all year and leave us alone. This is the last warning you're getting!" Nate commands in a voice loud enough to halt everyone in the room.

Thomas looks to the right to calculate the distance between Savannah and Nate. Looking once around the room to assess the crowd. As he brings his head back to Nate, his right fist follows and lands squarely on his jaw with enough force to make him land on the couch in the opposite direction of Savannah. He'll be out for a bit. Knowing no one at the party will come to Nate's defense, Thomas doesn't feel the need to watch his back as he picks up Savannah's limp body and carries her out of the room.

Thomas isn't as tall as the rest of the fraternity brothers, but he knows he is the strongest. 5'11" isn't short by any means, but he is compared to everyone's six feet plus height. Between helping out at Kate's farm on the weekends he goes back home and breaks from school, along with his use of the gym at the college, his frame is solid. He has always felt the need to stay strong. The school provides mental strength and his workouts provide the physical aspect. This sorority will surely suffer without his grade point average to keep them open. That's something he's counting on.

It took barely any effort to carry Savannah up the three flights of stairs. She's very petite, unlike Kate's muscular frame. Both of them are short for females. He wonders if Savannah has a feisty personality like her aunt. Does she get even like her aunt? He's never had a reason to get on Kate's bad side, he fears for the person who does. She's crafty when it comes to finding a punishment for someone who does not complete the work without a sound reason. The only reason he knows Kate is heavier is that he's had to lift her a few times to help her accomplish a goal. Now that Noah is at the farm, he's had to thankfully lift her less. Not that she's too heavy for him, he just doesn't enjoy helping her put herself in unsafe situations. She's Noah's problem now.

Walking through the doorway, he kicks it shut. He gently sets Savannah on the bed and tucks her in after taking off her heels. Such small feet. After placing a wastebin by the bed, he stops to look at her. She is incredibly beautiful. There's no wonder why Nate tried to add her to his count.

Now he needs to find the phone he accidentally left behind in his haste to leave before the party started. Coming to retrieve the phone was his real reason for showing up. Thankfully, he showed up just in time to prevent Savannah from a terrible fate. What would he have done if he came home to her on the couch after she'd been used by whoever wanted to take what they thought they were owed? Probably would have gone to jail for seeking a personal form of justice.

After a quick search, he finds it behind the end table and dials the intended number. As the phone rings, he turns towards the door to lock it. Hopefully, she answers the phone. He has no idea what he'll do if she doesn't. Probably call the cops. He'll call them anyways, but he would rather have her here when he does.

"Thomas? Is everything okay?" The woman asks with concern.

"Kate, we have a problem………"

Chapter Two

"Just pull up to the curb and park," Kate urges.

"It's a NO parking zone, they'll tow your truck," Noah informs as she bounces impatiently on the passenger seat.

"Look! They're getting ready to leave," she adds with a jab of her finger.

As Noah puts the truck in park to wait for the other car to load up and back out, Kate jumps out of the truck and throws the door closed. "Kate!" He scolds loudly as he watches her run across the yard to the front door.

"Excuse me, this party is by invite only," says a young man who's attempting to be a bouncer. He's tall but lacks the muscles needed to throw anyone out. At least that's the appearance he gives off.

"Ew," Kate blurts out in response to his statement as she assesses him. "Thomas invited me here," was the next response out of her mouth as she pushes her way through.

She really should have waited for Noah, but she is already anxious to get to Savannah. It took them two hours to get here from the farm. Noah made the argument that since she was safely in Thomas' room, they didn't have to speed like a lunatic. That was also why he dragged her out of the driver's seat. He knows her well enough to know she wasn't planning to listen. Such a shame since she could have shaved thirty minutes off.

Once Kate is clear of the doorway, she begins making her way to the staircase. Snickering at the sound of Noah attempting to persuade the bouncer to step aside. He could easily throw that guy to the side if he wanted to. His strength excites her. His ability to lift her as if she's as light as a feather makes her beg for more. Almost to the staircase and she feels a sharp sting on her ass. Turning to find the person who slapped her on the ass is a man with an unsightly fresh wound to his jaw. Not taking the time to put the pieces together, she simply looks over to find Noah who had seen the exchange. A simple nod to him and she is off to find Thomas.

Fuming at what he just witnessed happen to Kate, he has to remind himself he is only here to beat one man's ass tonight. Instead, he chooses a simpler route. Quicker than a cat's reflex he grabs the man's throat and throws him against the wall. "You touched my wife's ass. That was a BIG mistake you worthless piece of shit," Noah snarls as he continues to choke the man and his face begins to turn purple. "The next time a woman walks past you, keep your hands off of her."

The man struggles as he tries to remove Noah's hand from his neck. As Noah lets go of his neck and the color starts coming back to his face, he turns to see Kate running back downstairs with Thomas in tow. The man starts to gasp for air now that he's free of his hold. "What the hell man, I didn't know she belonged to anyone." At this point the room is silent. Music has been turned off so the last of the partygoers can focus on the events unfolding.

Noah takes a few steps to reach out to Kate, but she brushes past him while dragging Thomas along. Stopping in front of the man Noah just released, "this?" She asks Thomas while pointing at his unsightly face. A nod from Thomas is the only response she gets.

"What the hell, Thomas? Get out of my face," the man warns Kate.

"Nope! I need your words, Thomas. Is this the guy that had Savannah on the couch?" Kate demands while unsuccessfully trying not to direct her anger at Thomas.

"Yes, his name is Nate," Thomas replies quickly as if he's at the farm responding to her authority.

Back against the wall, but this time Noah has his forearm holding Nate against the chest. "Do you think you're a gift to all females? That they owe you some ass just because they walk in your presence?" He asks without wanting an answer.

"The number of women I've had would point to yes," Nate boasts with a smile.

"I'm going to throw up," Kate responds to his lewd comment.

Releasing the pressure on Nate's chest just a little to let his back off of the wall, Noah then shoves hard against his chest making Nate also hit his head. "Shut up," he growls.

"That chick wouldn't have had a single complaint once I was through with her. She'd be begging for more," Nate boasts with an even bigger smile on his face. "Now, let me go. You have whomever she is and there's not a scratch on her."

"Let him go, Noah," Kate agrees.

Stepping back as he starts to release Nate, Noah turns to Kate. Just as he's about to demand answers, Kate steps forward and quickly forces her knee into Nate's crotch.

"That's for slapping my ass," Kate explains with a grunt. Nate instinctively bends over and cries out in pain while attempting to hold himself together. Another quick movement and Kate grabs him by the head and shoves her knee into his nose. "That is for Savannah and any other female you've assaulted. How dare you," she explains as he falls to the floor.

"You bitch! You broke my nose!" Nate cries out. One hand holding his bloody nose and the other still cupping his crotch.

"Yeah, well guess what? It's assholes like you who bring it out in me. Thomas, call the police," Kate yells loud enough so the partygoers can decide for themselves if they want to leave.

"Babe, you couldn't just let me handle it?" Noah asks.

Kate shrugs, "I didn't know when the talking was going to end. I was much too impatient to wait any longer. Two hours in the truck, while you drove like a grandpa, gave me time to plot."

"Like a grandpa?" Noah asks while utterly flabbergasted. "I was driving ten over the limit the whole way here!"

"I could've gotten here much faster," Kate retorts.

Noah looks at Kate as though she has lost her mind. "I'm glad you didn't drive. Now I'm alive to witness just the kind of crazy I'm married to," he replies with a roll of his eyes but playfulness in his tone.

Kate is beaming with pride. Only a crazy man who loves his equally crazy wife would put up with such antics.

 Twenty minutes later……….

The police took statements from the witnesses who stuck around because they wanted to vouch for Thomas's heroism. Paramedics came and took Nate away with his police escort. Savannah slept like a dead person during the whole ordeal.

When it is finally Savannah's turn to be examined, the paramedics try their best to rouse her. The only response they receive from her is her snoring. Having no other choice, they decide to bring her to the nearest hospital to ensure she isn't needing her stomach pumped from what they assume is alcohol poisoning. They weren't pleased about Thomas waiting so long to call 911.

Kate, Noah, and Thomas follow the ambulance to the hospital. Kate decides to fill Dylan in on the situation. "Hey, you might want to meet us at the hospital near your house. We're following the ambulance that has an unconscious Savannah in it. Thomas found her at a party at his fraternity. We don't have any more details." Silence fills the line. So many things he isn't saying are an indicator of how pissed off he truly is. "I'll meet you there." His short sentence lacks emotion.

The four of them wait in the exam room while Savannah is wheeled off for tests. Thomas can't help but feel uncomfortable at the awkward silence happening in the room.

"What happened to my daughter?" Dylan asks with irritation.

He spoke too soon. "I came back for my phone and found Savannah sitting on the couch. I'm pretty sure she was drugged."

"Why was she even let in? Why does she even know where you live? Do you invite her there often?" Dylan begins with his anger.

"I haven't seen her since the wedding. I have no idea why she was at the party," Thomas says with a cool temper.

"What a good influence you are. Are you high as well?" Dylan says while walking toward Thomas.

Kate jumps in between the two. "Knock it off, Dylan. Thomas doesn't do those things. I've known him for years."

Instead of taking offense, Thomas just takes the brunt of the anger coming from Dylan. He would also be livid if he had a child in this same situation.

Dylan's misguided anger towards Thomas is not something Kate will tolerate. Thomas saved Savannah from unspeakable things. Dylan also needs to remember that Savannah is an adult who chose to show up at the fraternity, alone.

Savannah grew up entitled and sheltered from the harsh reality of life. Her choice in going there alone shows how naïve she is. In a perfect world, a woman wouldn't have to be so cautious about her choices. Unfortunately, we do not live in a perfect world. Kate doesn't even want to think about the kind of call she would have gotten had Thomas not been there to stop it from happening. Why did Savannah even decide to show up there?

Chapter Three

Damn, why does my head hurt so bad? Slowly, Savannah begins to open her eyes. Taking in the tubes and lines connected to her, she then begins to look around the room that she now knows to be a hospital. Thomas, Noah, Kate, and dad. Dad? Her eyes grow wide with fear. All four are asleep in their chairs. "What is happening?" She asks loud enough to wake everyone.

Thomas says nothing as he slowly leans toward her bed and pushes the call button. Still as handsome as she remembers. His black hair is in a mess. Probably a result of using the wall as a pillow. His bright green eyes were the first thing she noticed when they were introduced at Kate's wedding. He even smells good. Why does he have to smell so good? His face has stubble. Is facial hair a new thing? Maybe he shaved for the wedding. Kate and Noah sit up straight. Noah is holding both of Kate's hands with one of his while he is rubbing her back with the other. Dylan crosses his arms over his chest and puts on a face so stern that she already knows how unhappy he is. If physical smoke could blow out of his ears, it'd be doing so. Just like in the older cartoons.

"Thomas, why isn't anyone saying anything? How did I get here? Why are all of you here?" Savannah asks quickly and quietly. She can't help but stare at him. Might as well direct the questions to him since he's the least scary at this particular moment.

"Why indeed, Savannah? Why am I sitting in a hospital room at almost five in the morning when I could be sound asleep in my bed?" Dylan responds with more questions that have anger laced in every word he says.

"Dad, I have no idea why I'm here," Savannah answers with an attitude that suggests it isn't her fault.

Just as Savannah finishes up her sentence, the nurse walks in. "You're awake! How are you feeling? My name is Sarah and I'm your nurse."

"I'm very confused and no one is answering my questions," Savannah snaps.

"The confusion is normal. The doctor is right outside and I'm going to tell him you're awake. He'll be able to answer all of your questions," nurse Sarah responds sweetly.

As the nurse steps out of the room, Kate snaps, "your confusion does not excuse your attitude toward the nurse. Mind your manners towards the people who are only here to help you." Savannah rolls her eyes.

"Roll your eyes one more time at your aunt and you'll be wishing you were back asleep," Dylan growls.

A few seconds later, not giving Savannah a chance to respond, the doctor knocks and enters the room followed by nurse Sarah. "How are we feeling?"

Savannah sits in silence afraid of her father's wrath.

"I'm doctor Chandra. Yes, I'm aware it's a girl's name. The good news is that you're awake. The bad news is that without relying on the information from the people around you, you might never remember the last five hours of your life," Dr. Chandra informs.

Savannah's eyes grow larger than when she first caught sight of her father. "Can someone please tell me what's going on?"

"Gamma Hydroxybutyrate, which is commonly referred to as GHB, was found in your system. It explains your memory loss and the after-effects you're feeling. Do you remember who gave it to you?" Dr. Chandra inquires.

"No. All I remember is going to Thomas' house and not finding him. Thomas, are you the one who called my dad and aunt on me?" Savannah accuses.

Thomas sits in silence. This is not a road he wants to go down. He wants to be asleep in his bed. Sitting here being treated like a punching bag is not how he imagined spending his weekend.

"This man saved your life. You should be grateful he found you when he did," Dr. Chandra urges.

"I like this doctor," Kate declares. "Savannah, you need to be taken down a peg or two. You could've been raped or killed and all you're worried about is Thomas ratting you out? Shame on you."

"Dad?" Savannah looks toward Dylan.

"I'm so angry. It's best if I don't talk for the time being," Dylan admits. "You're in big trouble."

After about fifteen minutes of discussing with the doctor what the next steps for Savannah will be, Kate, Noah, and Thomas decided it was best to go home. Dylan is staying with Savannah. Although by the looks of it, she would have preferred he left as well.

"Thomas, how have you managed to keep up your grades while living in that dump?" Kate inquires on the drive to drop Thomas off.

"I'm hardly there. I spend most of my time at the library or gym. By the time I realized what kind of fraternity it is, there wasn't another place in my budget. I didn't have another choice," Thomas answers with sincerity.

"Your parents couldn't help you with another place?" Kate asks.

"They are doing more than they can to help pay for the school itself. I didn't want to add more to their plate. I'm sure they would've tried if they knew," Thomas answers as he looks out the window toward the sunrise.

After stealing a few glances from Noah, Kate speaks up, "You should have come to us for help. I know men are stubborn," she starts to say but is interrupted by a snort from Noah. After a glaring look at him, she continues, "BUT your academics are more important. We would have found you a safer place to live," she softens.

"She's right, Thomas, we're always here for you," Noah seconds.

"Say that again," Kate jumps in.

"Say what?" Noah inquires with a scrunched-up face.

"That I'm right," she beams.

"You're insufferable," Noah returns with an eye roll.

Thomas can't help but smile. Their loving banter reminds him of his parent's love, the kind that lasts. "I'll be home in two weeks. Can we discuss an hourly rate? I think I'll take you up on that offer since school is turning out to be more expensive than I planned."

Kate pipes up without hesitation, "absolutely!"

Chapter Four

It's about par to receive a punishment before she can explain the facts. It's even more upsetting that she can't recall the facts. Why did she go looking for Thomas at his fraternity? Not having his phone number explains why she didn't try to call instead. Why would she drink the alcohol that was offered? She's never had alcohol, nor the desire to try it.

Savannah is the eldest child. She has a younger sister that has a habit of getting into things she shouldn't. Being the eldest, it is always Savannah's fault for not watching Annabelle closely enough. The two-year difference seems like ten with how much more responsibilities Savannah has compared to her. The two never seem to get along. Annabelle thinks it's funny to get Savannah in trouble. Savannah resents Annabelle for taking advantage of freedom she's never had. Savannah follows curfew, but her sister does not.

Savannah's 5'1" petite frame is no match for her younger sister who already towers over her. Savannah did not get her father's height. Savannah has blonde hair and Annabelle has the most beautiful brown hair. Savannah has lavender eyes and her sister has brown. Her sister has a bigger bust size, but Savannah has always boasted about having a nicer ass. The two are forever competing over something or another.

As shallow as it sounds, the only thing that keeps her at home is her monthly allowance. As unfairly as she's treated in other aspects, her dad does spoil them in a materialistic way. Savannah's appearance reflects upon the family. Therefore, she needs to maintain it with the best clothes and accessories. Before their mom left them, they lived a simpler life without all the things that now consume their smaller-than-average home. A divorce is an embarrassment in her father's eyes and he seems to overcompensate for their appearance with stuff others covet. The shiny bandage over a disgusting wound won't last forever.

It's not the nice things that truly matter to Savannah, it's the money. Since she turned eighteen, her allowance has increased. She's been able to save quite a bit in a secret bank account. She hopes to save enough to go to college out of state or at least far enough away that her father won't want to visit so often and disrupt the life she's trying to make for herself. Her father promised to pay for college if she attends closer to home so she doesn't have to live in campus housing. He refuses to pay if she chooses a college out of his reach. As much as she loves her family, she's had enough of the control issues. He relishes on her relying on him to survive. Kate had the right idea moving away from it all.

One more week and his freshman year will be over. One more week and he'll be home safe and in his bedroom. Thomas has been counting down the days. He's packed every single item he won't need for his last week of school. His dad is coming this weekend to help him load up as much as possible to make his last day easier. Thomas only has a car to bring the last of his things back home and he doesn't want to make a second trip back to this shithole on move-out day. Nor does he want his parents to make a second trip.

As much as he loves school, his living situation is not ideal. This fraternity would be shut down if the dean could prove what's happening behind closed doors. Nate has already been expelled for what he did to Savannah. There was an investigation, but nothing incriminating enough was found to shut down the whole house. In the fall, Thomas plans to find an apartment off campus before all the good ones in his budget are taken.

As an only child, his parents help pay for the part of schooling his scholarships can't cover. They're far from rich, but he's never had to go without. His decision to become a doctor isn't a weight he wants his parents to bear financially. Thankfully, he worked hard in high school to get the scholarships he did. Otherwise, he would be in a disgusting amount of student loan debt by the time he is done with school. Still, he finds himself in need of extra cash on occasion. His parents are adamant about not wanting him to work part-time. They're afraid a job will make his grades suffer. He knows they would make an even bigger sacrifice in their lives if they found out he was working.

Thankfully, Kate has agreed to pay him at the ranch this summer. He normally volunteers to help out, but there's no longer any need to impress the college he's already in. He can save what he earns and use it towards the cost of his housing. If he's lucky, he can find a studio all to himself. After this fraternity, he's not thrilled with the idea of having more roommates.

Ever since the party he rescued Savannah at, the other brothers have been acting as if he no longer exists. The conquest Nate wanted to have with Savannah would have broken the tie between himself and Jack. Now that the parties are done, no one was declared a winner. Idiots.

For whatever reason, Thomas can't stop worrying about how Savannah is doing. Has she recovered from the experience? Will he ever see her again? Why does he care? Why has the memory of her in his bed seeped into his dreams? Well, sans the GHB in her system. Has she regained her memory? He needs to ask Kate what happened to her after they left the hospital.

Chapter Five

"Dad!" Savannah yells, "you can't!"

"You're right, I can't make you go. If you refuse, you'll be out on your ass faster than you can say 'I'm sorry,'" Dylan retorts in a calm voice.

There are times when Savannah thinks pushing her dad's buttons is a game. Now, is not one of those times. When her dad is yelling, she knows eventually he'll soften. Which doesn't happen very often, but it's a personal victory for her when it does. When he talks to her in a calm and normal voice that lacks emotion, she knows she's in for it. Their current situation is an example of it.

"Dad, I don't want to go live with aunt Kate," Savannah whines.

"Don't think of it as living with her, since that would mean you would have privileges. Think of it as community service. You are irresponsible, entitled, and have shown no remorse about what you have put us through," Dylan continues in his normal voice.

"For how long?" Savannah asks in defeat. Nothing she can say now will convince him otherwise. Arguing will only enrage him into finding further punishments.

"For as long as it takes to make you realize that life is not your plaything and that there are consequences for your actions," Dylan answers. "Pack your clothes and the necessities. Your aunt will be here in the morning. She's thrilled to have the extra labor."

Savannah has no more words. Slumping her shoulders in defeat, she heads to her bedroom to do as he says. Clothes and necessities? Where does she even begin? His definition or hers? Does she even own clothes for working at a ranch? Looking around her room, she is racked with indecisions.

The next morning……..

"Well good morning sunshine!" Kate greets with too much enthusiasm.

"Hi," Savannah returns weakly.

"Tough labor is not the end of the world. Cheer up, it'll be good for you," Kate tries to encourage.

"I've helped you before. It wasn't fun getting dirty," Savannah retorts. "It also wasn't fun dealing with those two guys."

"Well, before you were my niece who was visiting and earning extra money for whatever reason. Now you'll be at the farm helping without the special treatment. The jobs will be harder, dirtier, and the days will be longer," Kate explains in her management voice. "As far as those two men, Noah handled them. That sort of situation is never allowed."

"Dirtier?" Savannah asks with concern.

"This summer will be good for you. If you let them, the animals will teach you things. If you come into this with a bad attitude, you'll have bad days. Let the ranch humble you. I love and care for you deeply which is why I agreed to take you on. I wouldn't dream of doing this for anyone else. I know who you are underneath this exterior you've built. She's the woman I expect to see at the end of this," Kate ends with a heartfelt smile.

There's nothing Savannah could retort with. Absorbing all her aunt had to say despite the desire to argue that the woman she's referring to has been buried too deeply. She started digging the hole soon after her mom left. Never feeling safe enough to uncover her true self around her father's harsh personality.

The drive to the ranch seems a lot quicker than the other times she's been here. Being lost in her thoughts must have sped up time. Still trying to recall the night of the party and wondering if Thomas will be home for the summer. Also wondering if she can fake it well enough to go home sooner.

"I don't need to give a tour since you're already accustomed to where things are. You're taking the studio that used to be Noah's. There's a new mattress in there for you. No parties, drinking, or drugs. Your workday starts at seven in the morning, which is slightly later than the rest of the workers start, but you'll be staying until four," Kate begins to explain.

"7:00 a.m.? That's early!" Savannah whines.

"You're an adult. A real schedule will only benefit you," Kate replies while trying her hardest not to roll her eyes. "There's an alarm clock for you to set once you get inside. Your first day is tomorrow and 7:00 a.m. comes real early for those who aren't used to it," she continues to explain.

Savannah just listens. Taking the key to the studio from Kate's proffered hand while internally trying to figure out how to adjust to her new life on the ranch to fit her a bit more.

Kate helps Savannah with her bags. Dang, she has a lot of stuff. "All these are clothes and necessities?" Kate inquires after the fourth bag. She was talking to Savannah when Dylan loaded up the truck, so she hadn't paid any attention to it until now.

"Dad couldn't tell me how long I'd be staying," Savannah answers with a shrug.

"It's not a specific length of time. It has everything to do with you and your view on life. Your dad might've spoiled you to no end, but I sure won't," Kate replies sternly.

Savannah didn't respond to her aunt. Would her aunt even listen if she said that who she has pictured in her head is Annabelle and not her? Does she even know her brother treats his kids differently? Looking around the apartment she'll be living in, "pretty plain apartment," she says, feeling the need to make a smart-ass comment.

"Only the best for you," Kate retorts while heading towards the door. "Get settled in. I'll see you bright and early."

"Do you think you'll be able to help her?" Noah asks Kate in their bedroom.

"She needs to learn to help herself first. I don't think she's a lost cause. I just think it's going to take a lot of work. Dylan did her a disservice raising her as he did," Kate replies.

"Babe, this is a lot of extra work you're adding to your already full plate. How are you going to train her and work on the new projects you have planned?" Noah asks with concern.

"Thomas comes home tonight. He will be training her," she replies with a wink.

"What did he do to deserve that?" He asks with his brow in an arch in reaction to her wink.

"He's not afraid of her. She won't be able to run circles around him like she would with Archer. Archer has a soft spot for her. He doesn't like Dylan for whatever reason. Besides, I already spoke with him and he's up for the challenge," she answers with a suspicious smile.

"What are you up to?" He arches his brow even higher.

With an exaggerated show of shock, she responds with, "who, me?"

"This isn't my first rodeo, Kate. You're up to something. Don't tell me, I will figure it out." Instead of responding with words, she slowly begins to get undressed. Seductively peeling off her clothes one by one. "This level of distraction isn't fair," he says with a rasp in his voice as he's unable to take his eyes off of her.

She smiles as she begins to pull down her pants to reveal that she isn't wearing any underwear. Locking eyes with him as she begins to unhook her bra and slides it off. The hunger in his eyes is electrifying. Trying incredibly hard to contain her excitement, she slowly begins to walk over to Noah who's already on the bed. They've almost been married for a year and her insatiable appetite for him still hasn't seemed to calm down. He's quite delicious and she hopes it never will.

"Kate," he hoarsely pleads. Without saying a word, she straddles him. Placing a hand softly on each cheek, she pulls him into a tender kiss. "Not. Fair," punctuating between kisses.

"shhh," she croons playfully with a smile, "make love to me."

Growling in response while he throws her onto her back. There's no need to tell him twice.

Chapter Six

knock, knock, knock

"Savannah, wake up!" Kate yells through the door.

knock, knock, knock

"Just a minute!" Savannah yells from the bed while still under the blanket.

"You better not still be in bed!" Kate demands. It's her first day and she has the nerve to still be in bed. There's no doubt about whether or not she is, she knows her niece.

Savannah jumps out of bed to throw on a pair of jeans to open the door. Not even bothering with a shirt. A bra is fine to open the door for aunt Kate. Reaching the door, she throws it open to find Kate, Noah, and Thomas standing there. The three of them whip their head to find Savannah half-dressed and the only one to look away is Noah. Thomas leans against the doorway to peruse all of her while Kate marches into the apartment.

"I said 7:00 a.m! What about 7:00 a.m. sounds like 9:30 a.m.?" Kate demands.

"I was tired," Savannah answers with a shrug. "You don't need me that much if you didn't realize I was late for 2.5 hours."

"You are not the only person at this farm, Savannah. Animals expect to be fed on time. I cannot stop tending to them just because you're being a brat," Kate snaps. Would Dylan mind if she gave her a verbal ass-whupping?

"I came to make sure she wasn't going to murder you. I think in this situation she might be justified," Noah shouts with his back turned and looking towards the pasture.

"Can you please turn around?" Savannah snaps at Thomas.

"You opened the door like this. Maybe next time you'll wear more clothes," Thomas retorts.

Kate snorts in response. "You have five minutes to get dressed or I'm dragging you out as is. If you think I'm playing, try me," Kate glares before she leads Thomas away from the doorway and shuts it.

Savannah emerges five minutes later with the rest of her outfit on. Teeth brushed and a messy bun will have to suffice today. Who's going to see that she'll need to impress? Thomas seeing her in a bra was mortifying. He wouldn't even avert his eyes when she snapped at him. Was he looking for flaws to later throw at her?

"Thomas is going to be in charge of you. He'll show you the ropes and keep an eye on you. Archer is usually the one who trains, but he's on vacation. If you act up, I will find out," Kate warns. "There's no need to complain about the pairing, it won't help."

Instead of complaining, Savannah is already trying to come up with ways to make Thomas give up on this pairing. Archer would be a lot more fun to work with. He's always been her favorite. The summer she was helping, he was the first to witness and step in when the two gross men tried to manhandle her. She wasn't even eighteen yet. He threatened to bury them six feet under.

Noah and Kate went off to do their tasks as Savannah begins to follow Thomas to what looks to be the goat pasture.

"Count how many there are," Thomas orders.

"One, two, three, four, five……. thirteen," Savannah returns. Does he not think she can count?

"There is supposed to be fifteen at all times. Your first task is to find the missing two," Thomas explains.

"How hard can that be?" She asks rhetorically. She begins to look around without stepping anywhere. Soon, she spots something on top of the chicken coop. Walking closer to get a better view, she realizes one of the missing goats is on the top ripping the shingles off. "How did the goat get up there?" She asks in disbelief.

"That's her favorite spot," he answers with a smile.

"Well, how do we get her down?" She asks with her head cocked to the side as she begins to look for a solution.

"That, my dear, is what you need to figure out," he says with another smile. Normally, he would jump at the opportunity to wrangle them, but not today. He already spent 2.5 hours this morning working alone on their tasks. He deserves this moment of entertainment.

Savannah reaches the side of the chicken coop and looks around to figure out a solution. How did she get up there? She grabs a nearby crate to stand on, but she still isn't tall enough to get up. The fencing on the coop isn't sturdy enough to climb. There's a small ledge, but the goat couldn't have used it. Could she have?

By the time Savannah manages to get on top of the coop, the goat jumps off the other side. "Are you kidding me?" She yells at the goat. Hearing a chuckling sound nearby, she looks over and sees Thomas leaning against the nearby tree with his arms folded over his chest. The image would be picturesque if he wasn't so damn irritating. He's not even trying to look attractive and she has to force her eyes away from him. He must have shaved recently since his stubble is nowhere to be seen.

"Animals don't tend to do things just because you want them to. There's gotta be something in it for them," he educates.

"In it for them?" She softly asks herself. Jumping down from the coop, she makes a break for it to the break room. Running inside just long enough to grab two bananas off of the table, then back to the coop.

The goat is now sticking half of her body out from under the coop. "Sorry, lady, but your butt is too big to fit," she tells the goat as she's pulling her out from under it. Once finally free, she grabs the goat by her collar to gently lead her out of the chicken's yard and to her pasture.

He watches her closely. She is gentler with the animals than she is with people. Watching Savannah's tiny frame jump down from the top of the coop made him anxious. She did it just fine by herself. She got up faster than he thought she would. In truth, he didn't think she would've succeeded at all without his help. It took a lot out of him to not be a gentleman and help her get down safely. His mom would have scolded him for it.

Putting the goat into her pasture, she breaks off a piece of the banana to feed it to her. "Now, time for the next one," she tells herself out loud.

It took almost 45 minutes of walking around looking for the next goat only to find it in the barn eating hay. "You are not supposed to be in here," she admonishes. No help from Thomas as he follows her quietly the entire time. Now, he's leaning against the barn door with his arms folded over his chest like it always is. "A real gentleman would be helping her," she mutters to herself as she rolls her eyes.

She peels the rest of the banana and slowly walks towards the goat who's watching her while chewing on a mouth full of hay. Stopping just far enough away to reach the goat if it takes a step forward. She extends the banana out as a temptation. The goat eyes Thomas by the door, then back to her. Quicker than it took her to process the situation, the goat snatched the banana out of her hand and ran past Thomas through the door. She slipped on something and is currently lying face down on the barn floor.

Everything hurts. If I just lie here, will they leave me alone for the rest of the day? Fat chance. She lets out a loud groan as she slowly pushes herself off the floor. Looking down to find the culprit she slipped on, it becomes pretty clear when she sees the fresh cow pie with her boot print on it. Looking toward Thomas, she begins fuming. "Why did you just let it through? You could have caught it!"

"Why couldn't you be here at 7:00 a.m. to help out?" He asks in a calm voice.

"That has nothing to do with this current situation!" She continues to yell. Her annoyance increases because she can't get a reaction. He's calm, just like her dad. Comparing the two is oddly unsettling.

"It has everything to do with it. The people at this ranch work as a team. If you don't want to be a part of this team, then you'll quickly learn how hard it is to do things around here by yourself. Your attitude not only hurts you but others around you," he continues to answer in a calm voice.

"So, this is a lesson?" She asks in disbelief.

"Lessons are a part of life. The goat getting out was just a perfect teaching opportunity. Let's go. You still have one more goat to catch," he orders while gesturing with his hand for her to lead the way.

Scowling as she marches past him with determination. She'll get the goat even if it kills her.

Kate pokes her head out of the stall and looks at Thomas, "you know she's going to be pissed if she ever finds out that you let them out."

"I'm sure she will," he shrugs.

As she scans with her eyes for the missing goat, she soon spots it following Christian back to its pasture. No bribe, no lead, and no effort on his part.

Thomas stops beside Savannah to follow her line of sight and smiles. Another teaching opportunity has arisen.

"He's not even trying!" She whines.

"They love him," he says with adoration.

"So, they just follow him?" She asks with attitude.

"Why wouldn't they? He feeds them, plays with them, and makes sure they have plenty of water and toys. Christian is eleven years old and he already understands what it means to have something depend on him for their survival. The goats choose to love him. Just as the chickens do with Hazel and as the cattle do with Kate. Now come on, we have shingles to fix," he urges. Watching her grunt as she stomps off to lead the way. "Spicy little thing with a nice ass," he softly mutters to himself as he follows a few feet behind to get the best view.

Wondering how it would feel to have his hands grab hold if he picked her up. He shakes his head to get the image out and to focus on getting their work done.

Chapter Seven

knock, knock, knock*

"It's 7:05 a.m., Savannah, you better be awake!" Kate yells as she begins to unlock the door. There's silence as Kate opens the door. This time she is alone since Thomas is starting on the stalls that need to be mucked. There, still in bed, is a nude Savannah. She looks so small in the bed and it reminds Kate of the second chance she's trying to give her. Savannah is a good kid and she always has been. The choices she's been making lately are very unlike her and she can't continue down the path she's on. Her dad has shielded her from the reality of life for far too long. Giving her everything she's wanted without making her earn it. "Look at that cute butt!"

Savannah jumps from the rude awakening. "Aunt Kate, I'm naked!" she shrieks as she pulls the sheet over herself.

"It's not the first time I've seen you. You used to run naked throughout your house. I see your tushy is still as cute as ever," Kate teases lovingly. "Besides, if you were up and clothed on time for work, I wouldn't have seen it."

"What time is it?" Savannah asks while looking for the alarm clock. "Shit! I forgot to set it last night. I'm so sorry!"

"You better get a move on. Thomas is mucking the stalls alone and he's not happy about it," Kate informs with a smile.

"I bet he's going to punish me again," Savannah replies with an eye roll.

"A different person would've fired you. Seeing as how he's not allowed that option, I'd say you've barely just uncovered the surface of how creative he can get," Kate answers with amusement.

"I'll be dressed and outside in five minutes," Savannah answers while jumping out of bed.

Kate doesn't feel the need to respond with a comment, so she walks outside to give her some privacy. It's hard on her to be so firm with Savannah. All Kate wants to do is dote on her with love and understanding about the assault, but she can't. Savannah isn't showing the slightest bit of remorse.

"Four minutes and I even brushed my teeth," Savannah says while jumping out of the apartment.

"It's a new record, you should be proud. Although, tomorrow you should try doing something with your hair. That messy bun isn't fooling me," Kate replies with a tease. Savannah deadpans.

It's 7:20 a.m. by the time Savannah meets up with Thomas. Kate already walked off to do her work. Before she says anything, she looks at his profile from behind. The sweat is making his shirt stick to his body and the muscles on his arms are bulging and giving the appearance that his t-shirt is too small. "Look, I had every intention to be up on time. I forgot to set my alarm," she informs as she walks up from behind him.

"In that twenty minutes you were late, I've mucked four stalls. See if you can beat that," Thomas replies while handing her the pitchfork.

"Okay," is Savannah's only reply. She doesn't want to argue. She's too tired to deal with more repercussions from running her mouth.

Thomas gives a look of confusion in response to her single-word reply. There is no attitude, no complaint, just a single 'okay'? Who is this woman and what has she done with Savannah?

While watching Savannah begin to muck the stalls, he can't help but notice the tight pants she chose to work in today. Normally, he would think about how ridiculous it is that someone chose clothes they couldn't properly move in. Right now, he's enjoying the pants and how it's hugging every inch of her ass. Every bend forward makes her pants tighten even more. If they rip, he will have the best view. Her hair is up in a loose hold. A little tug and it will all come down. Another route would be to grab hold of the bun, bring her close, and tilt her head to the side to expose her neck. A nip here and there would bring her to her knees.

After forty minutes of very hard work, she finishes the fourth stall. "Done," she says while standing before him with sweat dripping from her. Watching the sweat drip slowly down her neck gives him the urge to blow cool air on it to make the hair on the back of her neck stand up. The idea of her nipples perking up from the chilling sensation is starting to make his cock hard. Seeing her in a bra yesterday allowed him the knowledge that she'd fit perfectly in his hands. Mouth. "Come with me," he orders after spending too long imagining the wicked things he would like to do to punish her for being late. He takes the pitchfork from her and sets it next to the stall she was just working on.

She dutifully follows without a word. Curious as to what other punishment he has in store for her. Chasing more goats? Maybe she'll be chasing chickens this time? As they walk into the empty breakroom, she looks around for potential things he's going to make her do as punishment. Holding a water bottle out for her is the last thing she expected. "This is for?"

"Drink," he orders.

"It's not even cold. Why do I need to drink it anyways?" Questioning with an arch in her brow.

"Your face is as red as a tomato and you've been sweating significantly, you need the water. Drinking room-temperature water allows your body to process it faster. Drink," he explains.

She looks at the water, then back at him. "Why are you being nice?" Asking with suspicion in her voice.

"I'm always nice," he answers with a shrug. His thoughts are wicked, but they'll remain as thoughts. This is his boss's niece after all.

"You weren't nice yesterday," she retorts.

"You needed to be punished for your behavior," he replies sternly. He can't punish her the way he'd like, so he has to be creative in a different way.

Opening her mouth for a retort, then closing it when nothing comes out. She glares at him and then opens the water bottle to drink it. Realizing how good it feels to drink the water, she begins to chug it. He quickly rips the bottle from her mouth and spills some down the front of her shirt. "Hey!"

"Drink slowly," he returns with a commanding voice. He watches the water sink into her shirt and makes the material stick to her breast. His cock jumps at the idea of her taking it off to dry faster.

Savannah scowls at him with an outstretched hand. Once he hands her back the bottle, she retorts, "you're so weird," then slowly starts to drink.

"Good girl. Once you drink all of it, I'll help you finish the stalls," he says while ignoring her comment.

'Good girl' doesn't sound like innocent praise. What's happening today? The way he is eyeing her is making her feel warm in the spots she reserves for behind closed doors. It's been too long since she has touched herself and he's making her ache and throb. She'll have to attempt to satisfy herself tonight.

Once 4:00 p.m. hit, Savannah was not thankful. Working distracts her from her thoughts. She doesn't have time at work to sit and try to recreate the scene from the party. She doesn't remember much more than arriving and asking for Thomas. She only envisions the parts others have told her. It's killing her that she can't even remember why she was looking for him in the first place. Other than Kate's wedding, she had never even talked to Thomas before. When she helped out at the farm before, she never even approached him. Never had a reason to. She was younger and had no interest in talking to anyone other than her cousins and Archer. She didn't even have his phone number. She only knew where to find him because Kate had mentioned helping him move into his fraternity. Kate mentioned how proud she was of him.

Other than the family dinner at Kate's, she's left alone too much. She has never liked being alone. For as long as she can remember, she's hated it. Now, it's for a different reason. Nights are filled with nightmares. Not of what happened, THAT, she would probably never recall. The nightmares are of her imagination running wild. A lot of them tend to involve her eyes being open and watching what was happening to her. In her dreams, Thomas never arrives to save her. Nightmares continuously wake her throughout the night. Leaving her exhausted and late for work. The first morning she turned the alarm off intending to be late because she needed more sleep.

This morning was an accident. She simply forgot to turn the alarm back on so she could be on time.

Walking through her apartment door, she heads straight towards the alarm. She's very determined to not receive any more punishments from Thomas. He is taking too much pleasure in punishing her. She's not trying to have an attitude or be mean, it just comes out as her shield. If she keeps up her attitude, she won't break down and cry in front of everyone. While growing up, her dad told her that crying is a sign of weakness. Never wanting to appear weak, she only cries behind closed doors.

"I wish I had a friend close by," Savannah admits regretfully to herself in front of the mirror. Walking away from it, she is determined to distract her thoughts. Time to settle the ache between her thighs. She has always found it weird to touch herself. Only does it out of need and never takes pleasure in admitting it. It takes forever to accomplish feeling satisfied. She always feels shameful after the deed. As if she is doing something she ought not. Always wondering if everyone has the same feeling. Never having enough courage to ask anyone about it.

Chapter Eight

Savannah surprises everyone by being in front of the cattle pasture at 7:00 a.m. Feigning a refreshed look with a little bit of product and a smile for Thomas. She slept like shit, yet again. She's been up since 4:30 a.m. but no one needs to know that. She doesn't need questions about something they're not letting her have a voice on.

"Well good morning sunshine!" Kate beams.

"Good morning," Savannah returns. The look of happiness on aunt Kate's face makes it worth dragging her reluctant ass out here.

"You and Thomas are going to scrub out all of the troughs. Make sure you rinse them well after scrubbing, Savannah," Kate orders in her management voice.

Thomas and Savannah gather the things they need to start the troughs in the cattle pasture. There are three large troughs spread out over 125 acres for the cattle. The farm is a total of 250 acres. Thankfully they don't have to clean the troughs for the bison. Thomas decides to wash the first one to show her how to do the other two. Washing and rinsing them properly will prevent the cattle from getting sick.

"Please get the hose ready," he tells her just as he's about to finish. It's a hot summer day, even as early as 7:00 a.m. He's all sweaty after only washing one. His cock jumps at the thought of watching her get sweaty again.

"Sure," she replies with a sinister grin he cannot see. After hooking up the hose, he says he's ready for the rinse. "Bad choice of words," she mutters to herself. Hose pointed in the intended direction and then she pulls the handle.

He had a feeling this would happen. She's been so well-behaved thus far. The feel of cool water against his sweat-soaked skin is incredible. It's just what he needed, although he won't admit that to her. Standing up against the water still blasting him in the back, he turns around. No expression on his face, just looking straight at Savannah who has a smile plastered from ear to ear. Now being sprayed across his chest, his shirt is sticking to every muscle in his chest and arms. Without saying a word, he starts to run toward her.

"OH, shit!" She exclaims while dropping the hose and then begins to run from him.

It wasn't long before he caught up with her. Grabbing her by the waist, he pulls her back to his front. Holding her tightly against him to soak her clothes with the excess water from his. As she begins to wiggle to try and free herself, he notices how nicely she fits against him. The feel of her ass perfectly seated in his crotch. If she continues to wiggle, she'll start to feel the evidence of his thoughts. To put a stop to it, he firmly holds her lower stomach with his right hand and wraps his left arm around both of her arms. "Stop moving," he says hoarsely.

"You're cold! Let me go!" She grunts while still trying with all her might to wiggle free.

"I'm just trying to share the experience you so kindly presented me with," he retorts while trying his hardest not to think about how easy it would be to slide his hand a little lower into her pants. To make her squirm in a whole new way.

This started as an attempt to engage him in a harmless water fight. She wanted to test if he can be playful with her. Now, Savannah is trying to wiggle free to escape these new sensations brought on by being this close to him. It feels intimate and it's making her body throb and ache once again between her legs. She's also pretty sure she can feel him growing against her. Wicked thoughts enter her mind to see how far she can push him. She stops wiggling and asks in a flirty manner, "so, Thomas, how much of a gentleman are you?"

"You have no idea," he replies with a husky voice. A deep groan follows.

"Will my captor at least allow me to face him?" She challenges him with a grin he cannot see.

Not knowing her intentions, he falls into her trap. He spins her quickly enough to still hold onto her. Now, her breasts are pressing up against his cold wet shirt. There's at least more room for his cock in his pants since he's not pressing her lower half against himself. Soon, her nipples will be hard enough to press into his chest.

"What does my captor intend to do with me?" She asks as she proceeds to look into his bright green eyes and bites her lip. She can hear him groan loudly in response to her words. His facial hair is starting to grow back in. She prefers him with hair on his face since it makes him look more mature.

Looking into her lavender eyes, he wants nothing more than to have his way with her in this pasture. Her nipples at full attention show just how cold she is. His cock jumps at the thought of warming them up with his mouth. Shaking his head, he begins to look for her intention through her eyes. Something is there that he can't quite put his finger on. Leaning lower next to her ear, he whispers, "what is it you're wanting me to do?"

Her eyes widen at the challenge. She has no idea what she wants. She didn't even think he would match her. Not knowing what else to say, she shrugs and replies, "kiss me."

He looks into her eyes once more. Not as wide as they were a minute ago, but still unsure. Kiss her? He's not kissing her when she lacks conviction. What is this woman doing? She shrugged as if it would mean nothing to her.

Thomas leans down a bit further and stops just before their lips touch. Close enough to feel her breath on his lips. "No," he answers swiftly as he picks her up by the waist and throws her over his shoulder. As he begins walking back towards the trough, she starts to fight in an attempt to be let down. One firm spank on her ass makes her as still as a statue. Almost to the trough and someone pipes up.

"What kind of fun are the two of you having?" Kate teases with amusement across her face.

"Aunt Kate, tell him to put me down!" Savannah finally says something. The nerve of him to carry her like a child who's throwing a fit. If he didn't want to kiss her, the 'no' would've been sufficient.

As soon as he sets her down, Savannah stomps off to the trough. The sight of her throwing a fit amuses him to no end.

"I'll do these myself!" Savannah shouts while rinsing off the trough he had finished cleaning. If she does it herself, he won't be close enough to touch her.

"Are the two of you having fun?" Kate asks as she leans in for only Thomas to hear.

"She's trying to make a game out of her punishment," Thomas returns. He doesn't want to be a part of her game. It wasn't fun in high school and it doesn't feel fun now.

"A little bit of fun is allowed. I'm not an actual warden, but I'll leave it up to your discretion. I want her to learn her lesson, but not hate the ranch in the process," Kate replies softly.

Thomas nods his head in response. He's not going to tell Kate about her asking for a kiss. It's not necessary to get her involved in something he can settle himself.

As Kate stands there watching Savannah struggle with the trough, she fights the urge to go help her. She needs to learn how to work through the challenges life will throw at her. The decision to have Thomas in charge of her was the best she could have made. As he climbs onto the fence to perch on top, she smiles. He's allowing her to figure it out on her own. Any of the other workers, including Archer, would've given in to help her. When will she learn she's directing her anger at the wrong people?

She quietly retreats to the house to have lunch with Noah as promised. As busy as life at the ranch has been lately, she always makes time to be alone with him. Her kids usually spend the day at their friend's house after their chores on the ranch. The house being empty, she can easily tempt him into having some dessert. Sometimes in the kitchen, but most of the time in the bedroom.

Chapter Nine

After a long hard year at school, Thomas deserves this chance to unwind. He was pleasantly surprised by how easily he was able to convince his parents to let him have the house to himself. They took a weekend trip to the city to ensure he has the privacy he wants. He was honest with them about what he has planned and promised no alcohol or drugs. Thomas doesn't partake and his parents know that. The three of them have an honest relationship and they talk about anything. His parents taught him that respect works both ways. That dishonesty isn't respectful.

He invited Kate and Noah from the farm, a few other neighbors, and some people he grew up around and went to school with. The last party he was at confirmed that Savannah is not responsible enough to be invited. Not to mention that he needs a break from her. They've been butting heads since they started working together. There's a considerable amount of tension that he can't do anything about.

The day they cleaned the troughs, she was doing great and they were getting along until he refused to play her game and kiss her when she didn't mean it. She spent the rest of the day stomping around. The next day she showed up for work on time, but she wouldn't talk to him. She followed his orders, but he wouldn't get a response. Rather than eat lunch with him, she chose to sit on her patio. He didn't even have to bother to disinvite her since she was ignoring him.

A few hours later and he found himself playing poker with his neighbors. His buddies from high school were bummed to find out that Thomas had no alcohol to drink in the house. They decided to stand around the kitchen island and eat the snacks while having a conversation. Kate and Noah said they would be here soon after Savannah shows up to watch Hazel and Christian.

knock, knock, knock

Thomas opens the door to find Savannah standing in his doorway, soaking wet from the rain. Skin-tight green t-shirt paired with a black miniskirt. He half expected her to be barefoot, but looking down he finds her in sandals. Hair hanging loose with water dripping from it. Cheeks that are bright pink resulting from the water beating down on them and piercing lavender eyes he can't seem to stop looking into even when they're arguing. The green shirt is making her eyes stand out even more. If she wasn't so damn irritating, he would find her irresistible. "What are you doing here?"

"I heard you were having a party," she answers with a shrug.

"You shouldn't be here. You haven't even learned your lesson from the last party you were at," he bites. His irritation stems from her being so irritating and his desire to punish her in ways that aren't fit for the ranch. Wearing this outfit in the pouring rain. She knew what she was doing by deciding to wear this.

"Are you honestly planning on sending me back out into the pouring rain?" She asks even though she knows he wouldn't. Kate told her that Thomas is a gentleman and always does what is right.

He stares long and hard at her. There's something in her voice that says she knows full well he would never turn her away after trudging in the rain. "When Kate gets here, she can decide what to do with you."

She puts on a devilish smile and walks into his house. "There are no other females here? This party just got even better," commenting loud enough for Thomas to hear as she continues to look at the group in front of her.

He rolls his eyes in reaction to her comment. Just as she was about to step out of reach, he grabs her arm and pulls her backward. "You are going to dry off before you continue into the house. You're leaving puddles everywhere," he explains as he leads her to the bathroom. Grabbing a large towel, he then throws it at her. "Do you need any help?"

"If you're wanting to touch me, you need to be more creative than that," she returns with a roll of her eyes.

"If that's the route I intended, you'd be begging me to touch you. I'm simply asking if you need any help as a good host would. I see you have it handled," he bites with irritation before he starts closing the door.

"I'm not a child," she bites back just as he shuts the door.

He keeps the door shut because he knows she is baiting him into another argument. Before he walks off he pulls out his phone to text Kate and inform her of his uninvited guest. Hoping she'll show up sooner knowing Savannah is here. He doesn't know how much longer his patience can be tested. Or how much willpower he has left to stop himself from fucking the attitude out of her. Maybe she just needs to get laid?

Savannah walks into the room full of people and makes herself at home. Picking two men who look to be about her age to converse with. Hoping to make Thomas jealous as she flirts with his friends while he's within throwing distance. She can feel the heat from his eyes while watching her from the dining table. He's not paying enough attention to the game and he'll lose his hand if he's not careful. There's something about him that makes her enjoy getting under his skin. Flirting with his friends Gabe and Leo seems to be grabbing his attention.

"As a female, what do you think it means when a female sits in a male's lap?" Leo asks.

That grabs her attention away from Thomas. "Depends on how she sat on your lap," she answers with a shrug.

"Facing me in a straddle position during our conversation. I didn't know where I was allowed to put my hands," Leo admits.

"Why didn't you just ask her?" Savannah asks with a puzzled look on her face.

"Then I'd look like someone who didn't know his way around a female," Leo responds.

"Pretty sure you already did. You would've come off better by just asking. She's a person. Treat her as such," Savannah advises. While she was talking, she heard Thomas snort at her advice. "Here, I'll show you. In fact, Thomas will help me show you."

"Will I now?" Thomas asks with hesitation.

"Yes!" Savannah affirms while pushing him firmly on the chair as she straddles his lap.

Thomas looks at Savannah with confusion. What is this woman's motive?

"It all depends on how someone is straddled on your lap. For example, sitting more at the edge of your knees while conversing could just be her being playful. For this, I would bet the safe thing to do would be to place your hands on her knees," Savannah explains while grabbing ahold of Thomas' hands to place them in the described spot. "If she sits more in the middle of your lap, you could safely assume that you can place your hands on her thighs. The top or outer portion."

Once again, she guides his hands as an example. As she grabs his strong capable hands, a shiver travels down her spine.

Thomas is carefully watching Savannah's movements. How she trembles while moving his hands to the correct spot. A tremble only he could feel. Not one significant enough for anyone to see. She's avoiding eye contact. A nervous person would dart their eyes quickly. All of her actions can only mean one thing and he's going to push her to her limits to prove it.

"If she sits close enough for you to be intimate, well, I'll let your imagination run wild with that one," Savannah jokes.

"I can explain that one," Thomas pipes up. "If she sits completely on your crotch," he continues to explain while propping Savannah where she needs to be, "especially if she's wearing a tiny skirt like Savannah is, you can move your hands along her legs until you reach her ass. Grabbing a cheek with each hand and pulling her even closer, like so," he instructs along with his movements. As he begins pulling her closer, his suspicion is verified. Panic spreads across her face and her eyes give her away. "If you can't handle it any longer, this is the next step," he says as he stands up while holding her even tighter against him. Holding her firmly, he begins to walk out of the room.

"What are you doing?" She asks in a panicked whisper as she wraps her arms around his neck and legs around his waist.

"Just helping you prove your point," he returns. Holding her in place with one arm while he opens his bedroom door is effortless. It also helps that she's holding onto him as if her life depends on it. Kicking the door closed, he walks over to his bed to lie her on top of it. While hovering over her, he grabs both of her hands to hold above her head, making her chest puff out. Not a peep from her so far, just frantic eyes watching his next move. Firmly in place, he uses his free hand to place softly on her neck and tips her head up and to her right. Leaving the entire left side of her neck exposed, he brushes his nose along her soft sensitive skin with his hand still around her neck.

She has no idea what he's doing. They are in a room away from everyone and he hasn't let go of her. She's too excited by what's happening to even ask. He hasn't tried to undress her and it's making her curiosity get the better of her. Feeling his lips accidentally graze her neck makes a soft moan escape her lips.

Dramatically inhaling her scent, he continues to brush his nose along the left side of her neck until his lips become dangerously close to her ear. Softly whispering, "you are playing fast and loose with something selfish men covet. Lucky for you, I don't seduce virgins."

"Who says I'm a virgin?" She asks while trying to sound as if she still has control of herself.

"Your everything gives you away. Most of all your eyes." He nudges her legs and they open. "Good girl. I'm always in control of my actions. Even when a beautiful woman sits on my lap in a tiny skirt," he says as he looks down to see her underwear, "and barely concealing underwear." He takes his hand off her neck and slowly trails it between her breasts, across her stomach, and wraps it around her waist to pin her down. Taking his thumb, he applies pressure as he grazes her hips. He then reaches down to use his index and middle finger to lift her underwear starting at her perineum. With his knuckles, he starts to slowly graze her skin. His fingers are slightly apart as he begins to move towards her entrance, pulling her thong along with him. Reveling at how wet she is just from his simple touches. Still moving his fingers upwards, his knuckles slightly dip inside of her making her gasp. "Fuck," he groans. He continues to graze his knuckles until he reaches her clit. Trapped in the gap between the two knuckles, he swirls them in a circular motion. After hearing her moan, he reluctantly leaves that spot as he continues to pull her underwear along with his fingers. "Even when you're so fucking wet and a tug of your underwear gets lost between your lips," he says with a straining voice. "The power you think you have over me is only when I allow it," he says while he looks into her eyes. After briefly viewing his handiwork, he goes back to her neck. This time, to gently put his lips on the sensitive spot behind her ear and places a light kiss. "You are powerless right now and I can tell it excites you," he whispers before letting go and pushing himself off of the bed. Turning quickly so she won't see how hard he is from touching her.

She is too stunned to find a response to what just happened. Continuing to lie there with her hands above her head long after Thomas left what she now knows to be his room. Why did that excite her as much as it did? Up until he picked her up, she thought she was in control of the whole thing. To find out he was in control by letting her do those things is a game changer. The scariest thing is that she was willing to let him do whatever he wanted to her. His hands on her made her tremble with the desire for more. When he removed his hand, it made her ache from the loss of his touch.

"Dude, that was fast," Gabe snorts. "Did you at least give her a chance to finish?"

Thomas stops dead in his tracks and glares at Gabe. "You know my one rule. Don't break it."

"It's been a long time since I've watched Thomas kick someone's ass. Please break it," Leo urges Gabe while barely containing his laughter.

Just then, Kate walks through the front door alone. "Where is she?"

"She's in my bedroom. Can you please take her home?" Thomas asks.

"Gladly!" Kate shouts as she briskly walks to his bedroom. She opens the door to find Savannah laying under his covers playing on her phone. "What the hell do you think you're doing?"

"Warming up because I'm cold?" Savannah retorts.

"Get up, we're leaving! You were supposed to hang out with your cousins. They were looking forward to it and you let them down. I'm very disappointed in you!" Kate roars.

As Savannah gets out of bed Kate notices her outfit. "You walked over here in the rain in that?" She asks in disbelief with eyes as wide as an owl. "Thankfully, Thomas is a gentleman and I can trust him to watch over you. You don't know anyone else here. What if another incident happened? You barely have anything on and it's raining!" She doesn't even recognize the woman in front of her. "Why did you even pack an outfit like that? Planning on mucking stalls in that?"

"Why do you have to be so mean about it?" Savannah asks while she looks at herself in the mirror.

"Mean? No one in their right mind would wear that outfit in the pouring rain. You walked almost a mile to get here. Are you trying to get sick so you can call out?" Kate yells in anger.

"You can't get sick from being out in the rain," Savannah replies with a surprising amount of sass.

"No, but you can sure as shit get hypothermia. I'm going to say this one last time, knock off the attitude. You don't have a leg to stand on when it's you who's treating everyone so poorly," Kate seethes. Savannah gives no response. Kate walks over to the chair Thomas has a mound of clothes on. At the top of the pile is a hoodie. Grabbing it, she orders, "put this on."

Savannah obeys and follows Kate out of the bedroom door. Not wanting to make eye contact with anyone, she keeps her eyes on the back of Kate's head.

"Bye, Thomas. Thank you!" Kate shouts as she walks out the door with Savannah in tow.

Thomas watches as they leave. Savannah is swimming in his hoodie and the sight of her in it makes him oddly happy. Tomorrow is going to be interesting. Probably more awkward than interesting. At least he gets to sleep in for a bit. Hopefully, Savannah will quell her anger toward him by the time morning comes. Knowing for sure she isn't too happy he called Kate on her. What the hell was she thinking wearing that outfit? Gabe and Leo immediately swarmed her, wanting to be in her favor. What did she think was going to happen by sitting on his lap?

"Is she seeing anyone?" Leo asks.

"No. She's off limits," Thomas bit off.

"I told you he's into her," Gabe says to Leo.

"She's in my charge at the ranch. It's strictly professional," Thomas retorts.

"Is what just happened, professional? It sure didn't look like it to me," Gabe teases as he dodges the look Thomas is giving him. "Don't hit me."

"Then knock it off," Thomas warns as he turns his chair to get back to the poker game.

Once they get in the car and begin to head home, Savannah pipes up, "Thomas isn't as innocent as you think he is. I don't think he falls into the gentleman category either."

Kate whips her head to look at her. "Elaborate, please," she says while trying not to sound demanding.

"He picked me up by my ass and brought me into his bedroom and then pinned me to the bed," Savannah simplifies.

"Did he force himself on you?" Kate asks even though she's afraid of the answer.

"No. He said he is always in control and doesn't seduce virgins," Savannah explains with an eye roll.

Kate let out a breath she didn't even realize she was holding. Internally praising Thomas. "Well, thankfully you're still a virgin. People in general can only be pushed so far. You're not always going to run into people like Thomas who can control themselves. That frat party is a good example. Some people will use any excuse to take advantage. I don't need another phone call where I'm scared half to death and the worst possible scenarios run through my head. Thomas saved you from the unthinkable. I know you like him, but being mean or using your body is not the way to go about getting his attention. He's a very smart young man, just talk to him."

"I don't like him like that!" Savannah exclaims loudly.

Kate rolls her eyes. "Life isn't like the lie parents tell their kids when someone pushes them down at the playground. With that lie, you learn to project flirtation in hurtful ways. Or worse, you accept mean behavior as affection. It's terrible advice to tell someone that the other person is being mean because they like them. Sometimes, people are just mean. Don't be a mean girl, Savannah. It doesn't suit you."

"You give advice differently than daddy does," Savannah confesses.

"Well, we are different people," Kate answers with a smile. "You owe your cousins a night to hang out."

"Yes, aunt Kate," Savannah acknowledges softly.

It's still pouring outside, so she pulls up as close as possible to Savannah's apartment to let her out. "Sweet dreams, Savannah," Kate bids.

"You too, aunt Kate," Savannah returns. She jumps out of the truck and runs to the safety of her porch.

Kate watches to make sure she gets inside safely before she backs the truck up. "That girl still needs a lot of work," she admits to herself out loud.

Chapter Ten

"Damn it, she's late again!" Kate shouts in frustration.

"Give her a rude awakening. That might teach her to be on time," Noah pipes up.

"That's a good idea," Kate replies, then pauses for a few minutes to think. "Thomas!" She yells across the field. As Thomas approaches, Kate informs "Savannah still hasn't shown up." Thomas was granted permission to be a few hours late since he asked beforehand. Savannah wasn't granted such a privilege.

"But it's almost ten, how could she possibly be sleeping in this late?" Thomas questions.

"Because she's a turd. Please take this spare key and go wake her up," Kate orders. Thomas takes the key without a word and walks towards the set of apartments.

"I thought she was naked the last time you woke her up?" Noah asks.

"Maybe she'll have clothes on for this rude awakening," Kate answers with mischief in her smile.

"I see what you're doing now," Noah returns while raising his left eyebrow. Kate simply smiles in return. She's playing matchmaker and he thinks it's going to spell disaster.

Thomas knocks twice, then unlocks the door and walks into the apartment. Savannah is in the kitchen facing the wall. Barely there shorts that have her ass hanging out and a see-through shirt.

"Kate, I just can't face Thomas after yesterday. I'm too embarrassed," Savannah says loudly while still facing the wall preparing her breakfast.

He closes the door without saying a word and leans against the wall to enjoy his view. Just recently he felt that nice ass while she was straddled in his lap. Now, he gets to see it with exiguous clothing. Assuming the white t-shirt is see-through in the front as well, he can't wait until she turns around. The tease of a view is much more exciting than her being fully naked. He can still use his imagination, which he prefers. His imagination couldn't be contained during his dreams last night. The sight of her in his bed is ingrained in his memory. A memory he doesn't know if he wants to shake. She irritates him immensely, so why is he drawn to her?

"Aunt Kate?" She questions as she turns around. As soon as she sets eyes on him, her eyes grow wide and she freezes in place.

Smiling that his assumption is correct. He can't quite see the color of her areolas, but they're darker than the white see-through shirt. The lighting in her apartment isn't the best and he now understands why her curtains are closed.

"What are you doing here?" She demands softly. She hasn't quite unfrozen the volume of her voice. He heard her frustration. What must he be thinking?

"You greet your aunt in that?" He returns with a question while using his right hand to flick at her outfit. He approves as long as he's the only one privy to the sight. The thought of Gabe or Leo seeing her in such an outfit sparks a bit of jealousy.

Oh, is he uncomfortable? I can use this to my advantage. "What's wrong with what I'm wearing?" She asks while doing a slow spin.

"I can see through your shirt. Kate would approve?" He asks with a brow in an arch. Still leaning against the wall while he positions one leg in front of the other to hide his desire.

"You've spent too long in the country," she retorts with an eye roll. "I'm over eighteen, I can wear whatever I want. If you don't like it, there's the door," she adds nonchalantly as she spins back to prepare the rest of her food.

"Never gave my opinion of you in the shirt. I simply questioned you greeting Kate with your nipples at full attention," he replies calmly.

"She has nipples also. I'm pretty sure she knows what the female body looks like," she retorts with a snort. Slowly spinning to face him once again, she begins walking towards him, "Does. My. Outfit. Make. You. Uncomfortable?" She asks while punctuating each word with a step closer, watching as he straightens his stance.

Standing before him, Thomas can now see exactly what color her areolas and nipples are, Nipples are pink with darker pink areolas. Another reminder of how innocent she is. He shouldn't want to fuck her until her innocence fades away, but he does. He won't. Even if she tempts him at every turn. "Savannah, I warned you yesterday," he replies in a husky voice.

"Are you really in control, Thomas?" She asks while lifting her shirt up and over her head. Standing there in just the tiny shorts her ass is hanging out of, with breasts fully exposed to him. Challenging him to react. This is not something she's ever done before. She's never even shown more than what a bathing suit shows to the opposite sex. There's something about him that makes her step out of her comfort zone. She's broken up with guys who've asked for less than what she's freely giving him.

He looks her up and down, stopping at her nipples which are standing at attention in the center of her perky breasts. Her perfect breasts. They look so much better without the constraints of a bra. If he was a weaker man, he'd have his way with her. She's toying with him and he knows it. He wonders how she would feel being toyed with. Reaching his arms out, he puts a palm onto each waist. Slowly moving his hands along each side of her body without breaking contact. Reaching her breasts, he takes his thumbs and traces the underside of both breasts, purposefully avoiding her nipples and the majority of the breast itself.

He can hear her pants of desire. Can only imagine the things she's feeling between her legs. How wet she must be. He moves his hands around to her back. One hand at the small of her back, the other moving upwards towards her hair. It took very little effort and pressure to pull her closer with one hand. Hearing her gasp at the quickness. The other hand sinks into her hair and pulls her head backward exposing her neck once more. "Always," he returns in a straining voice. The feel of her bare breasts against his t-shirt is tempting him more than he's letting on. Although, if she was more experienced, she would be able to hear the lack of conviction in his voice. It would be much easier to give in to the temptation if he didn't know she was toying with him.

"Savannah, I'm not a toy you can pick up and replace as you desire. Stop challenging me to a game you have no idea how to play," he demands while gently letting go of her to ensure she isn't going to fall. Stepping away and exiting her apartment so quickly you would think it was about to burst into flames. "Damn her," he mutters to himself as he storms off.

Feeling incredibly rejected, she runs to lock her door before she bursts into tears. With tears pouring down her face, she walks over to her bed to curl up inside her blanket and proceeds to cry into her pillow. Is she that revolting that he can't even be tempted when she's almost naked? The food she was going to have for breakfast is now wasted since she lacks the desire to eat. Reaching for her phone to message Kate. She better tell her she's not coming in. Hopefully she'll accept the reason. "I can't come in today. I need a mental and physical break from Thomas. Can I please spend the day crying in bed?"

"Fine, but you're coming to the campfire tonight at 7:00 p.m. Your younger cousins want to roast marshmallows with you. No buts about it," Kate replies instantly.

"See you then," Savannah quickly replies before the bigger tears start pouring out. He's right about her not knowing how to play the game. She just didn't think rejection from him would hurt as much as it does.

Twenty minutes later……

"Thomas!" Kate yells while signaling with her hands to come closer. When he gets close enough to conversate quietly, she asks, "what happened with Savannah?"

"She makes it very hard to be respectful towards her. I'm trying, Kate, I really am," Thomas blurts out with frustration.

Trying very hard to not jump to conclusions, Kate takes a big breath, "can you please elaborate?"

"She keeps throwing herself at me like it's a game," he says with more frustration. Realizing this is his boss, his eyes widen. "I'm sorry. I shouldn't have said that to you. I promise, nothing happened."

"I understand she can be frustrating. I appreciate your honesty and now I fully understand the text she sent. She won't be in today. Do I need to find another person to supervise her?" Maybe she shouldn't have sent him to her apartment.

"Not unless she asks you to. I can handle it," he answers with conviction.

"She'll be at the campfire tonight. Is that going to be an issue?" She feels the need to let him know she'll be in attendance in case he wants to change his mind.

"If it is, I won't stay long. I'm stoked Archer is coming home today. What did you mean you understand her text?" He wonders what transpired over text once he left. Maybe he should relinquish his responsibilities over her. He doesn't want this to jeopardize his ability to work here

"She plans to spend the whole day crying in bed. Which in girl language means she's feeling rejected by you," she replies honestly.

"Shit. I'm sorry, Kate," he says while now feeling like shit. He shouldn't have stooped to her level and played her game. He should have been better than that. He was raised better than that. She's so damn infuriating that he loses his ability to think straight.

"She's a grown woman who needs to be taught there are consequences to her actions. She likes you. She just has a shitty way of showing it. You're under no obligation to do anything with this new information. She might be a brat, but she's still my niece. I appreciate your restraint around her. All I ask is that you don't take something you can't give back unless it is something you both want. She has no idea what she's doing by tempting you," she answers with more honesty than she probably should have.

"I know. I'll let you know if she becomes too much to handle," he returns. Does she like me? If that's true, then she does have a shitty way of showing it. Has she thrown herself at the other guys she's liked? If so, then how is she still a virgin?

"That's all I ask," Kate answers with a smile. It's time to have a deeper conversation with her niece. She needs to figure out what's going on. Dylan's plan isn't working and it might be time to change how she's doing things. Why does Savannah think throwing herself at Thomas is the best way to get his attention?

Chapter Eleven

All day in bed has done nothing to better her mood. She doesn't want to go to the campfire knowing Thomas will be there. She'll make an appearance for the sake of her younger cousins, but there's no guarantee on how long she'll stay. Sometimes, she lets her attitude take control of her actions. Seeing him in her apartment this morning irritated her. He had the nerve to let himself in. He should have taken the hint when she didn't come to answer the door. She also shouldn't have pushed his buttons by taking off her shirt. The rejection stung immensely. The first time she makes a move and gets shot down.

While getting dressed, she becomes thankful for the cool night. Sweat pants and a hoodie will be comfortable as well as serve a greater purpose. It will cover as much of her body as she possibly can. Feeling rejected, she's also feeling self-conscious about not being attractive enough for him. She doesn't need more of Thomas treating her like a child who doesn't know what she's doing. Even though she has no idea what she's doing, she's not a child and it doesn't make her feel great when he throws it in her face. She doesn't know if she can mentally take any more rejection. She was never good enough for either of her parents. Not being good enough for a guy she likes is taking too much of a toll.

She doesn't know when she started to want Thomas for more than a friendship. They argue a lot, but there seems to be something between them. Something keeps pulling her towards him. Maybe it's just her that feels that way. She sees him and wants to be near him. Wants to be in the safety of his capable arms.

Kate always has the nicest campfires. Her fire pit is large enough for all of the employees and the kids to sit around comfortably. Her favorite part of the campfire is the seats. Multiple two-person seats are situated close enough for conversation, but not too close that someone can't have privacy if they need to have a quiet conversation. They are carved out of old logs and have been treated to make sure they don't decay with the abundance of rain they receive in certain parts of the year. The circle is large enough to sit on the opposite side of the campfire from Thomas and avoid conversation with him. After she humiliated herself, she wouldn't blame him if he wants to avoid her as well.

As she begins to walk across the field, she becomes even more thankful for her decision to wear her boots lined with fur. The rest of them are used to this weather, so she'll look overdressed. None of that matters to her when she wants to be as comfortable as she can in an uncomfortable situation.

Scanning the bodies around the campfire, she sees uncle Archer. He's home! She's missed him dearly. Ugh, he's talking with Thomas. She'll have to contain her excitement and talk to him when Thomas has moved on. A waive will have to do if he ever looks in her direction. Thankfully, Hazel and Christian are already on the opposite side, away from the adults.

"Hello the two of you," Savannah greets her cousins.

"Savannah! Took you long enough. Christian is challenging me to a marshmallow-eating contest. Tell him no," Hazel explains with an eye roll.

Savannah laughs. It feels good to laugh. "I don't feel like being sick all night with an upset stomach, so I think I'll pass, Christian," she says with a smile.

"More for me," Christian says with a shrug of his shoulder.

"Please don't puke either. I'm sure your mom isn't in the mood for cleaning it up," Savannah advises him.

"I won't," Christian muffles with a mouth full of marshmallows.

Hazel and Savannah laugh simultaneously. She can always count on her cousins to make her laugh.

Thomas looks in the direction of the laughter and finds Savannah with the kids. He's not sure he's ever heard her laugh before. A smile he's seen on a few occasions, but never a laugh. Watching her laugh is mesmerizing. At least her cousins can cheer her up. The sight brings a smile to his face.

Archer follows his line of sight. "Kate told me what you did for the family. Thank you, Thomas. Savannah is a very special person to me."

His attention is pulled away by the sound of Archer's voice. "You'd think I did something terrible from how she's been acting. That isn't the same person I met at Kate's wedding. She was shy and quiet. Now, I can't seem to figure her out and it bugs the crap out of me."

"What she went through was a scary ordeal. The world is a different place for females than it is for males. Are you sure she's not acting up out of fear? If she appears tough, she might believe people won't mess with her anymore," Archer answers. "Kate does that. I wouldn't be surprised if that's why she's acting up."

"So, what do you suggest I do?" Thomas asks.

"Let me talk to her. I'd hate to give you the wrong advice," Archer answers.

"I'll go talk to Kate so you can go say hi. Something tells me she's trying to steer clear of me," Thomas admits as he heads toward Kate and Noah.

Walking over to the kids, Archer greets her, "hey, kid!"

"Uncle Archer!" Savannah greets him as she jumps out of her seat and into his arms.

"Let's go for a walk and talk," Archer suggests as he wraps her in a tight embrace. Savannah nods and they both walk off in search of privacy. "A little birdie told me that you've changed. Why would they say that?" She shrugs her shoulders in response. "I'm going to ask you some questions. Please answer with honesty," he informs while taking a good long look at her. She still seems like the little girl he met 6 years ago.

"Okay," she agrees meekly.

"How have you been sleeping since the frat party?" He asks in a soft tone.

"Oh, those kinds of questions. Honestly? I haven't been sleeping much. When I do, it's horrible. I'm always so tired, but I'm afraid to sleep," answering somberly.

He softly nods his head. "Why did you go to the frat party? It's not like you to go to an event like that."

"It took me a while to remember it. I went there looking for Thomas to give me a ride home. I was on a horrible date and decided I couldn't even make it through the dinner. Kate had mentioned a few months ago that he lived at that specific frat." A pause is taken while she tries to regain her strength Bowing her head as she adds, "I thought it was safer than walking home. Now everyone is mad at me and I was only trying to do the right thing." Finally feeling safe enough from the comfort of Archer, she begins to cry. Archer has been the only one to ask her these questions without exuding anger.

"Oh, kid," he whispers as he pulls her into a hug. Giving her a loving kiss atop her head, he adds, "you gotta tell Kate.

Your aunt will understand your fears better than you think she will. Once you do, she'll understand your anger."

"No one lets me get a word in," she answers between sobs.

"I'll be here to hold your hand," he says with a smile. "Stay here, I'm going to go get her."

"Now?" She asks with wide eyes as panic starts to set in.

"Yes, while it's raw. It's important that you close this wound," he explains with a giant bear hug.

Five minutes later Kate and Archer walk up to a teary-eyed Savannah. "Archer, you've been here a few hours and you're already making someone cry?" Kate scolds.

"Kate, she needs your ears and not your mouth," Archer says sternly. As he walks closer to Savannah, he grabs her hand to hold. Giving her the strength she needs to have this important conversation.

His stern voice and few words said everything she's been fearing. Without a smart-ass remark, Kate listened. She listened to the fear, anger, exhaustion, and heartbreak her niece has been feeling without someone in her corner. Without knowing her aunt has been in her corner this whole time.

Kate heard Dylan's side of the story and accepted his plan to bring her around. She shouldn't have waited so long to get Savannah's side of it. All the anger she's been projecting now makes sense. Wrapping Savannah in a tight hug, she whispers, "I love you so much, kid. I'm sorry I didn't let you have your voice." Once she finishes her words, Savannah begins to cry harder. Kate holds onto her until she begins to settle down. "I think you owe Thomas an apology. You don't have to share the details. He doesn't deserve your past attitude. Although I understand the reason behind it, he still deserves one."

Savannah looks up into Kate's eyes and nods her head. "Can he walk me home?" If she's going to close the wound, it's best if she does it all at once.

"You'd have to ask him," Kate answers with a shrug. "I don't foresee him denying you that request, but it's up to him. The worst he can do is say no."

The three of them walk back to the campfire. Knowing there are obvious signs she's been crying; she puts her hood up. Standing alone near the campfire, she watches Kate approach Thomas who's standing near the other two men Kate employs. Unable to hear the words that are being exchanged, she notices Thomas look in her direction and nods to Kate before he begins to walk over.

Thomas has no idea what Savannah wants. Kate was very cryptic with her words. Reaching Savannah, his eyes immediately scan her face. Her beautiful lavender eyes glossed over from what he can assume were tears. Her red face is also an indicator that tears were recently present.

"Can you please walk me home?" Savannah asks softly.

He's taken aback by the question and her tenderness. What's going on? "Of course," he finally replies.

They start walking to her apartment in complete silence. Thomas doesn't know why he was asked to walk her. It's not that far from the campfire. Maybe a five-minute walk if the pace isn't brisk. Maybe she's afraid of walking at night in the country?

Reaching the front door, Savannah finally turns to him. Her glossy eyes are more visible with her porch light. Eyes that are finally showing a hint of softness. Thomas can't help but reach out and run his hands through her hair as he lowers her hood and stops briefly with one hand to cup her cheek. The touch was too quick for her to react. If he was to put money on it, she was about to lean into his hand from the way she closed her eyes.

"I'm sorry, Thomas. For all of it. The attitude, being late for work. Most importantly for throwing myself at you. You didn't deserve it no matter my reason behind it," she says sincerely.

"Rumor has it that you like me. Is there any truth behind it?" He needs to know if her aunt is just projecting her opinion.

"There's no reason to discuss that. It's clear to me that I repulse you. With my attitude, I don't blame you," she answers softly as she unlocks the door and steps into her apartment.

"Whoa, wait a minute," he says with outrage as he pushes his way into her apartment. "Why would you say that?"

"This morning is a fine example of that," she admits sheepishly.

"When I thought you were toying with me?" Asking with anger.

Nodding her head. "I'm sorry," is all she was able to get out before more tears begin to roll down her cheeks. She turns away from him before he can see the evidence.

"Savannah, look at me," he demands. Still looking away, she shakes her head. "Savannah," he says while stepping forward. He grabs her arm and spins her around. Just then, he sees it, the tears she was trying so hard to hide from him. Trying her best not to make eye contact, she looks to the floor. He pulls her into a hug and nuzzles the top of her head. "Please don't cry," he whispers. Simply because he has no idea what else to say. If this was a movie, he would kiss her. Knowing she would take it as a pity kiss since she's crying, he opts out and chooses to hold and nuzzle her instead.

The longer he holds her, the more she leans into him. His tenderness is making things better and worse at the same time. Even though she would like to stay in his arms, she can't. The fact that he still hasn't denied that she repulses him is running through her head. Ruining the moment she could be having if she would just stop her negative thoughts. "I'm tired," she says softly.

"I'll leave and let you get to bed," he replies while pulling away from her. Fighting the strong urge to kiss her anyways. He doesn't want her to be sad. He wants her to go back to the campfire and continue to laugh with her younger cousins. A slight pang of jealousy hits him. He has never been able to make her laugh.

"Okay," she says softly. He still hasn't denied it. He's leaving without any hint of him wanting to stay with her. His outburst isn't an act of denial. The outburst could easily be his outrage at getting caught.

As Thomas begins to walk back to the campfire, Hazel runs past him toward Savannah's apartment. He never realized what a fast runner she is. Must take after Kate. Watching her knock swiftly, Hazel lets herself in. Thinking nothing of it, he walks back to where Kate, Noah, and Archer are standing.

Before she could even answer, "come in," the door flew open. In comes Hazel like a ball of energy.

"Mom said that you and I need a sleepover. Also, she said that we can sleep in as late as we want. She never lets me sleep in," Hazel adds with excitement. "So, scoot over!" She exclaims as she starts pushing Savannah's butt to one side of the bed.

"All right!" Savannah exclaims. Hazel is small but mighty. She could've easily pushed her completely off the bed. Leave it to Kate to know that she needs company while she sleeps. Even if it is in the form of Hazel. For a brief moment, she thought Thomas was coming back to her. "At least she didn't send Christian. He'd never let me sleep in."

"I know! He never lets me sleep in either. He is so annoying in the morning," Hazel returns with an eye roll.

"Good night, Hazel," Savannah manages to get out before she falls asleep. So quickly she didn't even hear Hazel's reply.

"What was that about?" Thomas asks once he reaches the group.

"Savannah needs someone with her tonight. I wasn't sure how late you were going to stay. I bribed Hazel to stay up and wait for a bit. Told her they can both sleep in tomorrow," Kate replies in a normal voice.

"Didn't know how long I was going to stay? You thought I might spend the night with her?" Thomas questions with caution. What kind of guy does Kate think he is?

"She needs a friend to comfort her tonight. You're adults. It's not like I'm going to come barging in with questions," Kate replies.

Thomas pulls back. "She was crying! I'd feel as if I was taking advantage."

"You know, I knew I liked you for a reason," Kate teases. Thomas keeps surprising her and she's liking him as a prospect for Savannah more and more. Noah and Archer laugh at her comment.

"Goodnight, weirdos," Thomas replies as he walks off into the darkness toward his car. Was Kate suggesting he would have sympathy sex with her virginal niece? She knows she's a virgin, right? What a memorable first time that would be for either of them. He's never had sex with someone while they were crying. He is not sure he could even get it up while tears were streaming down her face. He would be too disgusted with himself after they were finished. Doubting he would even be able to finish in the first place.

Chapter Twelve

It's been a few days since the campfire. Things between her and Thomas haven't been argumentative, just awkward. Neither one of them has brought up their conversation. Savannah isn't sure of his reason, but she doesn't want to feel rejected again. She doesn't want his reasons or false denials.

Hazel only spent the night once and they slept in until past noon. Savannah slept hard. When she woke up starving, she was very surprised that Hazel was still asleep. That girl was taking full advantage of her only day to sleep in. Either that or Hazel stayed up late watching television while Savannah slept so hard, she couldn't hear. Either way, she was thankful for the security of having another person next to her.

Despite Hazel's reluctance to stay another night, she has been on time for work. Hazel doesn't want to be away from her bed unless she's promised to sleep in. Which is understandable. Hazel isn't interested in doing so without Savannah divulging why she doesn't want to sleep alone. It's not normal for her to ask her cousin to spend the night.

Lost in her thoughts, she wasn't paying attention to the fact that Thomas stopped working. A little nudge from him brought her out of it. "What?"

"Savannah, I was talking to you," Kate replies.

"Oh, sorry," Savannah replies as she turns around to face her aunt.

"Savannah, go to the feed store with Thomas and get some liquid colostrum," Kate orders.

Savannah's eyes lit up. A chance to go shopping? It doesn't even matter that it's only a feed store, she needs some retail therapy. "Anything else?" She asks eagerly while straightening her posture.

Kate chuckles. She knows exactly why Savannah is excited. "Don't take too long. The orphan will be here within the hour. We need to make sure we have what it needs."

Savannah gasps. "A baby? I'm so excited!" She squeals with delight.

"Don't get too attached. It'll be a tough road the next few days whether or not it will even survive," Kate tries to explain without too much sorrow for the orphan. She has experience in losing a few calves. Although, no matter how much she tries to not get attached, she always cries when a baby dies.

"Okay. Thomas, let's go!" Savannah urges while tugging his arm.

With a roll of his eyes, he follows. Watching her run to the car makes him laugh. Watching her turn around and scowl about the fact that he didn't run with her, makes him weirdly happy. She's in a good mood. Impatient, but good.

"Hurry up, turtle man!" Savannah shouts. Why isn't he going faster?

"I'm going as fast as my turtle legs will take me," Thomas retorts.

"Is that your first attempt at a joke? It was awful," she scolds.

Chuckling at her. Finally reaching the passenger door, he unlocks the car. He could've opened it from where Kate is, but then he would never have gotten to her door in time to open it like a gentleman.

She eyes him cautiously while he opens the door and gestures with his arm for her to get in. "Why are you being nice to me?" She asks with suspicion written across her face.

"I'm always nice. I always open doors for people," he answers with his brow in an arch.

"Oh. I could get used to this," she teases with a smile.

"No one has ever opened doors for you?" He asks while taken aback.

"Other than aunt Kate, no," she answers with a shrug.

"What kind of guys do you date? Holding the door open is the bare minimum of expectations," he replies with annoyance on his face and in his voice.

"I don't date much. Not everyone is jumping at the chance to get in line," she admits softly.

Closing the door for her, he stands there in disbelief. Savannah is prettier than all the girls he went to school with. Even his friends asked during the party if she was available. He warned his friends that she was off limits. What kind of idiots did she go to school with? Is that why she kept throwing herself at him? Does she have no idea what to expect or how to act around a guy?

The drive to the feed store was quick and quiet. He sat stewing about the info she shared before they left. He can't quite wrap his finger around the reason it bothers him so much.

She has never been to a feed store before and it's very new and exciting. Smells like animals. "Baby chicks!" She squeals. "Twenty-five cents?" She asks in disbelief. "You can buy a baby animal for a quarter?"

Laughing at her. "They're cheap because you can't always guarantee they'll make it to adulthood. You buy a bunch in hopes it increases your odds," he explains as he watches her lean closer to the babies.

She scrunches her face at his explanation. What could he possibly mean by that? Then it hits her, "oh." While Thomas went in search of the colostrum, she began exploring. It is the quickest she has ever walked around a store. She wants to see everything while respecting their time limit.

All he can see is her head bobbing up and down quickly along each aisle. Does she not think she can come here again? He chuckles at the absurdity of it. She's acting like an animal who's been let out of a cage for the first time. It didn't take long for him to find the colostrum. After paying for it, he yells, "let's go!" No response. "Savannah? Are you playing with the chicks?" He yells while searching for her. Nope, not near the chicks. Where is she?

"Thomas, honey, I'm over by the chicken feed," she shouts.

Why did she just call me, 'Honey'? Walking towards the chicken feed, he finds her cornered by two familiar-looking men. "Savannah, we gotta go!" He shouts impatiently.

"I'd love to, but they won't move," she gestures to the two men.

The two men turn around to look at Thomas, then waive. "We just wanted to talk to her, no harm done," the taller man says.

"Please let her pass, we really must go," Thomas instructs while trying to sound as calm as possible. These two idiots used to work for Kate. Their employment was short-lived and he never cared to ask why. Also, the two men cornering her stir up some anger. Jealousy? He wants to barge through and beat them for trapping her in a corner. Just then, the two men decide to part to allow Savannah to pass and she hurries through them. Making herself as small as possible while avoiding contact as if her skin would catch on fire. Running to him, she then wraps her arm around him as she urges him to move with pressure. He wraps his arm around her to play his part until they get to the passenger door. Opening the door for her, he teases, "here you go, honey."

She ignores his comment with a smile. When both are safely inside locked doors, she turns to him. "Thank you for playing along," she says with sincerity.

"Honey? It felt like my mother was calling me," he snorts.

"It was the first thing that popped out of my mouth. I regretted it as soon as I said it," she explains with annoyance in her tone.

"What did they want?" He inquires without trying to sound jealous.

"For me to relay a message to Kate. It was weird. 'Tell Kate we know about the owner of the ranch.'" She replies with a shoulder shrug. "I never wanted to see them again. Kind of freaked me out being corned by them."

"What is your aversion to them?" He asks out of curiosity while shifting in his seat. It seems he had the right of it to be angry at them for cornering her.

"They got a bit handsy the last time I was helping at the farm. Wasn't quite eighteen yet, not that it mattered. Aunt Kate fired them over it," she answers then shudders.

Why does the thought of someone else putting their hands on her make him jealous? She's not even his and he has no claim on her. He didn't respond to what she said. There's no way he could react without showing his anger. She would just ask why he was so angry about something that happened in the past. Although, he has every right to be angry at someone putting their hands on a minor.

As soon as they pull up to the farm, she sees it in Archer's arm currently being carried to the barn. It looks so tiny in his arms. She shrieks in excitement and jumps out of the car with the colostrum in hand and runs toward the barn. "Can I feed it?" She eagerly asks. She wants everything to do with this calf to help it survive.

"Sure, let me show you how," Kate answers.

Once Savannah is shown what to do, the rest is up to the calf. Encouraging it to suckle is difficult at first. The poor baby is so exhausted and weak from the lack of nourishment. Once a bit of the colostrum made its way to its belly, there was no stopping it. The baby drank the whole bottle and starts begging for more. Once the calf had its fill, it collapses onto the floor. Time for a nap after a full belly. Savannah patiently sits by the calf with a blanket over it to keep it warm. Admiring the cuteness. "This is probably the cutest thing I've ever seen," she whispers.

"We need to decide on shifts for the baby. Feedings and ensuring its health doesn't decline," Kate states.

"I'll do it all," Savannah replies while eyeing the sleeping calf lovingly. It's all black, just like Kate's other cows.

"It's a lot of work. You'll want breaks," Kate advises.

"I can do it. I'll even sleep in the stall if I must," Savannah informs.

"All right, this calf is your responsibility. Let us go over the feed schedule and how to care for it," Kate replies with a smile.

Thomas and Savannah listen to the care instructions. The feeding schedule, what to look for in case the health declines, and how to watch for scouring. They also learn how to check the calf's body temperature if need be. "I'll commit to this with her," he tells Kate.

"You don't think I can do this?" Savannah asks while clearly showing offense with her entire body.

"It's not all about you. I want to have this opportunity also. I've never had an opportunity like this before," Thomas retorts.

"Oh," Savannah replies softly.

"It's settled. Thomas and Savannah, his life depends on you. No pressure. Please don't kill each other in the process," Kate teases. The fate of the calf isn't completely on them. There could be an underlying reason why the seasoned mother rejected this baby. It's quite common for the mother to reject a baby that won't live long without human intervention. Sometimes it's best to let nature takes its course. Then again, we're a stubborn species.

"His? It's a boy?" Savannah asks in excitement.

"Yes," Kate smiles.

"Oh, there's something I need to tell you," Savannah says to Kate. Looking back at the calf while wondering if she can leave him alone for a brief minute.

"He'll be okay for a few minutes while we talk. Besides, Thomas is right here," Kate encourages with another smile. It's adorable how protective she already is over this new baby. I hope he makes it.

The two of them step outside of the barn to talk about what happened at the feed store. Before she met Noah, Kate would've been worried about the thinly veiled threat. Now that he's by her side, she has nothing to worry about. People would be stupid to ask for money now that it also belongs to him. She doesn't spend the energy hiding the owner of the ranch anymore. She doesn't go around shouting the information, but she also doesn't continue with her story. "They're trying to blackmail me since they found out I own the ranch. Well, now it belongs to Noah also. They're idiots, just ignore them," she shrugs it off. "Just make sure they keep their hands off of you. Tell them your uncle with kick their ass again," as she laughs.

"I never knew you hid that information in the first place. You're such a strong role model for us four," Savannah says with admiration.

"When did you find out?" Kate asks with curiosity. She never knew Savannah was aware of her ownership. Now she's beginning to wonder if Dylan let any hints slip up around anyone else.

"I've known since the beginning. It wasn't hard for me to piece that puzzle together," Savannah says with a smile.

"Smart girl," Kate says with approval. "Go take care of that baby. You and Thomas don't have to worry about the other tasks. I will make sure they're covered. The first three days are the most crucial."

"Yes, aunt Kate," Savannah says with a nod then runs back inside the barn. The baby is still napping and Thomas is on the floor next to it. There's something sweet about this picture. She doesn't say anything to interrupt the moment. Instead, she sits on the other side of the sweet baby and places her hand over Thomas's to hold it.

Neither of them said anything while the baby slept, which wasn't for very long. They spent the next few hours encouraging the baby to walk around the stall. Once he got the hang of it, they took him outside to the small pasture. When it started to get late, they took the baby back to the barn to get settled in for the night. There are a few nursing mothers in the next few stalls and it's like the baby can sense it. It keeps crying out for its mother and the sound of it is breaking her heart. "This is so sad," she says to Thomas.

"I know. It's a shame that none of these mothers are keen on adopting an outside baby. The mothers that usually do, can't at the current moment. As much as the baby would choose otherwise, it's up to us." Like all species, not every mother is willing to accept an outside baby. The ones who do are incredible.

She can't take the crying any longer. "Thomas, let's bring the baby back to my apartment after this last feeding. I can make a cute bed for him on the floor. Also, my apartment is warmer than this lonely stall," she says to try to convince him.

"Where am I to sleep? I guess I could sleep on the floor. It'll be cleaner than sleeping in this barn. Hopefully," he teases. "Give me ten more minutes and he should be done eating."

"I'll go and get the apartment ready," she says with excitement. The more she thinks about it, the more she knows her idea is so much better than what they were going to do. A bed. A nice warm bed. On the way out of the barn, she grabs a stack of blankets reserved for the animals.

Twenty minutes later......

Knock, knock, knock

"A little later than you said, but the timing is perfect. I just finished," she says while opening the door for Thomas and the calf.

"I wanted to make sure he went to the bathroom before I brought him inside," he explains.

"Genius!" She praises. She didn't even think about that aspect. "Good thing there are no carpets or rugs in here."

Thomas settles the calf onto his makeshift bed and he goes right to sleep. Standing up and looking around the apartment for his best sleeping options, he spots a chair.

"You can sleep in the bed next to me. I promise I'll behave," she suggests. "You just need to take a shower before you get in. You stink," she adds to tease.

"We both stink. Do you think it'll be a safe idea?" He asks hesitantly.

"There's no other man I'd trust more to be in my bed," she answers quietly. "I'll get you something to sleep in. Your clothes are too filthy for my bed."

Taking the first shower quickly to try and be considerate and not use up all of the hot water. Normally, she stands under the hot water until all of her fears melt away. She chooses to get dressed before leaving the bathroom. Fully clothed in matching sweatpants and a sweatshirt.

After Thomas finishes his shower, he emerges from the bathroom in her size-too-small sweatpants. Every inch of his lower half is being hugged in them and she can't seem to peel her eyes away. "Jeez. That is a man's size and they're baggy on me. You must be a lot bigger than I thought."

"I think you're just a lot smaller than you let yourself believe," he teases. "They're fine for a night."

Shirtless and in tight pants. Savannah now needs to try her hardest to be good. Which will be hard with her imagination running wild. She's never seen him shirtless before. A wet shirt sticking to his skin is the best view she had gotten up until now. Shirts do not do him justice. His muscles look much bigger without a shirt. Her eyes begin to follow the trail of hair that leads from his stomach to his southern region. He is wearing pants much lower than he should. Just a few more inches and she wouldn't have to use her imagination. Looks like he has it right above his pubic hair. He must have been watching her since he cleared his throat to grab her attention.

"What side of the bed do you prefer?" He asks while laughing on the inside. He took too much pleasure in watching her peruse him. He needed to distract her before she could witness his excitement in the already too-small pants. Even if he slightly grew, she'd still notice.

"I've never had someone other than Hazel or my sister share a bed with me. I'm not sure I have a preference?" She answers with a blush as she fixates her eyes on the mattress. She can't look him in the eyes while divulging that private bit of information.

Instead of responding, he chooses the side closest to the door. They both quietly settle into bed under the covers. There's only one blanket to share between them since Savannah made sure the calf is plenty comfortable. Trying very hard to not touch him to respect his side of the bed, she starts wondering if the calf would sleep through the night if she slept next to it.

He can tell she's nervous. She is unnaturally stiff and it can't be comfortable. "Seeing as the baby has all the extra blankets, you need to scoot closer so we can keep each other warm." Slowly, without a word, she begins to scoot closer. He takes the initiative and rolls onto his side. Turning her, he pulls her into the spooning position and she willingly lets him mold her to him. With a kiss on the back of her head, he whispers, "sweet dreams, Savannah."

"Goodnight, Thomas," she says in return. Weirdly enough, she let him rotate her. She trusts this man who is not hers to be in this bed. As if she knows what it's like to be in bed with any man. Safe in his arms, she melts against him. The goodnight kiss was a nice touch. Everything about this feels right and good. She really should halt her thoughts since this situation is only temporary to take care of the calf.

Chapter Thirteen

Savannah slept like a rock next to him. Head resting on his chest in the comfortable dip between his pec and shoulder. Opening her eyes, she sees her leg draped over his thigh and her hand over his cock. Well, it would be if the sweatpants weren't in the way. Carefully moving her hand to not wake him, she places her hand on his stomach. His rock-hard stomach. It's a good thing her hands are warm. Cold hands would've made him jump from the rude awakening. To her surprise, his skin is soft and smooth. She always had the notion that men have rough skin. Her dad has rough skin, so she just assumed it was a guy thing. Her thoughts begin to wander and she begins to fight an overwhelming urge to run her hands across the rest of his torso to test if it feels the same.

As her eyes wander back down to his cock. she can't help but wonder if it's painful to be straining so hard against his pants. So hard, the waistband of the pants is slightly lifting. Not enough for her to view his flesh, but enough that her hand could easily slip through. She could never be so bold as to follow through. Her imagination, on the other hand, can't be tamed. Just because she hasn't let someone have all of her, doesn't mean she wouldn't want to with the right person. Someone gentle and patient enough with her lack of experience. Someone who hopefully wouldn't make her feel like an idiot for her inexperience. Could that be Thomas? She promised to behave. Her eyes and imagination will have to suffice.

Thomas has been awake for quite a while. Reveling in holding her in bed. He woke up when her hand slid from his chest to his cock. She nuzzled him even tighter and let out a soft moan. Originally, he thought she was awake when her hand slid down to touch him. He instantly became hard at the contact. When she didn't move again, he knew she was asleep. The smell of her is incredible. He was becoming aroused just from her scent. Even in his sleep, he could smell her. The scent seeped into his very naughty dreams. When she touched him, he was no longer able to conceal his desire.

He's been hard and awake this whole time. Once he felt her wake up, he immediately closed his eyes. Too curious as to what the reaction to her hand placement is going to be. Is she going to freak out over her actions in her sleep? He feels her lift her hand to his stomach, which isn't very far from her original position. Close enough to his waistband if she still wants to try something. He feels when her eyes wander back down to his cock. The slight tilt of her head made him smile. He wants to make his cock jump to get a reaction out of her, but he can't. There's no room to move in these tiny pants. "You didn't have to move your hand," he teases with a smile while his eyes are still closed.

"How long have you been awake?" She asks as she tries to push off of him in surprise. He's holding her too firmly to be successful.

"Stay, this is comfortable," he replies while purposely ignoring her question. "I have a very good idea what your moan would sound like. You gave me a brief insight while you were asleep. It was different from the noise you made on my bed." Wondering if her moan was in reaction to a dream about him. He's felt her delicious wetness before. Maybe she's even wetter from her dreams. The desire to find out is an itch he can't scratch. An annoying tease.

She buries her face in her hands in embarrassment. "I'm sorry," she muffles through her hand. Why won't he let me go so I can retreat to the bathroom?

"For what you did in your sleep? No harm done. Well, a little. I was disappointed you were sleeping. Out of the vast things I'm into, somnophilia is not one of them," he says nonchalantly.

She has no idea what that even means. She'll have to look it up when she has a moment to herself. "Does it hurt?" She asks while still hiding her face. She feels compelled to know, which is why the question jumped out of her mouth before she could resist.

"Gotta be more specific than that," he teases.

"That. The straining against the pants," she elucidates softly.

He lets out a deep throaty chuckle. "It would feel better without the constraint, that's for sure," he pauses, "I noticed you were watching my cock earlier. What were you thinking about?"

She successfully rolls away onto her side in reaction to that question. Could she be any more embarrassed than she is now? She grabs a pillow and covers her face with it while her arms begin holding it down.

Rolling onto his side to reach, "don't smother yourself. While I do enjoy a light choking, necrophilia is definitely not a fetish of mine," he teases while taking the pillow from her. Using his strength, he pulls her body until she's lying on her back. Using his right knee, he lays it over her right leg to pin her down. Her face is beet red, her eyes are closed, and she is trying with all her might to hide from him. "Savannah, please answer honestly. I know you're a virgin, but have you ever touched someone's bare cock before? Or even seen it?"

She feels his hardness pressing against her. Feels the wonderful sensation it's bringing to her insides. With her hands now covering her face, she shakes her head violently from side to side.

"That's a new one," he remarks to himself. "Do you even want to?"

She stills herself. What does he mean by that? He can't possibly think she's into girls from how she acted when she first got here. "Meaning?" She asks through her hands.

"Meaning that I'm not ashamed of mine. If you want to explore, you just have to ask. No need to feel embarrassed by your curiosity," he explains. "I can't believe you never satisfied your curiosity with a previous boyfriend."

"You'd let me touch it? Without expecting all of me?" She asks nervously as she slowly begins to pull her hands from her face. Why the change? He wouldn't even kiss me the other day when I asked. Is this due to their proximity in bed?

"All of you? You can do as you please and I'll follow your lead. But you have to ask," he replies in a rough voice. The anticipation of her hands on him is making him strain more. It's becoming painful and he hopes she'll agree and release him from the restraints. What he wants, is to hear the words come out of her mouth.

"I can't say things like that," she goes back to hiding her face.

"Yes, you can. Say it. May I touch your cock. You can trade cock for dick if that word is better?" He suggests as he grabs her hands to pull them away from her face.

She has no idea whom she woke up next to, but this side of him is exhilarating and nerve-wracking at the same time. She has never asked for something like that. "Can I?" She asks softly.

"Can you what?" He teases. He wants to hear the begging from her innocent mouth. Immensely enjoying the fact that his cock will be the first she's touched.

"Touch you?" She quietly asks without conviction. Why is he being so difficult? He already knows what she wants to do.

"Touch where? My arm? Sure," he continues to tease. He'll play this game until she says what he wants to hear.

"Can I touch your penis?" She asks just above a whisper.

"We'll work on the wording next time. Yes, feel free. It won't bite," he answers with a smirk. He might bite, but his cock won't.

Next time? She looks at the bulge straining against the pants. Where does she even begin? Is it delicate? What if she touches it too roughly? So many things she should ask, but doesn't have the nerve.

He watches her hesitation. "Pull it out. You won't break it," he encourages patiently. His mind is screaming the opposite.

"Can you close your eyes? I don't know if I can do this with you watching," she explains with heat creeping up her neck. She knows her face is blushing.

"Watching makes it even better," he explains in a husky voice. He takes her one hand and guides it through the gap in the waistband. Groaning once her soft hands make contact.

She traces her finger along his cock, "it's so soft!" Finally gaining the courage, she grasps it.

Thomas bites his fist when she finally grabs hold. Who knew her inexperience would make the sensation unbearable? Restraining himself from touching her despite everything his inner monologue is telling him, he uses one hand to hold her in a cuddle position while the other grabs the sheets for purchase. As he watches her attempt to pull it out, he fears she'll let go of the waistband and it'll snap back on him. He uses his free hand to grab his pants and pulls them down so she can have free range of the whole thing.

The moment his cock sprang free, it was all she could look at. She takes her fingers and lightly traces the shaft until she reaches the tip. Looking closely, she sees a small pool of liquid at the top. She runs her fingers through the slick liquid and rubs it between two of her fingers. He groans in response. "Did I hurt you?" She quickly asks while pulling away.

"Not even close," he strains. He grabs her hand and firmly places it around his shaft. With his hand over hers, he shows her how to stroke him. He wants very much to give in to the voice inside of his head and move his hand from the cuddle position to her breast. She hasn't asked him to. Hasn't permitted him. He doesn't want to scare her away from her curiosity.

She is watching the tip of his cock like a science experiment. The more she moves him up and down, the more liquid begins to pool. Eventually, that pool travels down his shaft onto her hand. Without thinking much about it, she decides to taste it. Taking her tongue, she licks the pool of liquid from the tip of his cock. It isn't bad. Why did her friends complain about it so much?

"Oh, shit!" He exclaims when she licks the tip. He begins grabbing the sheets even harder to prevent his hands from making her take the whole thing in her mouth. He never thought the exploration of her hands would also include her mouth.

"Should I stop?" Hesitating after his 'oh, shit.'

"Only if you want to," he strains. Please don't stop is what he honestly wants to admit.

She brings her mouth back to his cock and begins by placing kisses on it. Testing the different sensations her lip has versus her tongue. This is enjoyable. Would it be as enjoyable doing this with another person? Is he the reason she's enjoying herself?

Moo

She sits up abruptly. "I forgot the baby was here," she looks at him with wide eyes. Good thing the calf can't rat her out to Kate.

With closed eyes, he struggles to form words. That damn calf is going to kill him. "I guess he's ready for breakfast," he weakly responds. "I need to use your bathroom to finish."

"Oh!" She exclaims. "Um, go ahead," she gestures with her hands toward her bathroom. Not fully understanding what he means by finish, but she kind of has an idea. She jumps out of bed to go tend to the calf while Thomas does what he needs to do to 'finish.' What would've happened if the calf didn't interrupt them? How does it make her look that she's touched his penis, but has yet to kiss him? Maybe he doesn't want to kiss her? Maybe he is just being a friend who's helping her satisfy her curiosity?

Chapter Fourteen

Thomas has spent all day with Savannah and the calf who seems to be thriving under their care. Even within the proximity, he can't stop thinking about her. Finishing in the bathroom brought him little satisfaction. He wants to continue what they started this morning. Hopes she'll suggest another night in her apartment to keep the baby warm and safe. Two wins with that suggestion. What started as a friend helping another friend with her exploration, soon turned into something else entirely. At least for him, it did. Most people, himself included, did their experimenting in high school. She was one of the few who did not. Thomas wasn't lying when he said he wasn't ashamed of his. He grew up in a household that didn't shame others for what comes naturally. He doesn't want Savannah to think her thoughts are anything to be ashamed of.

She's a grown woman and it's hard for him to fathom that no one has ever allowed her the opportunity to explore. Thinking back to her question, maybe she's been afraid that a little play means she would have had to give all of herself. Maybe a past boyfriend encouraged her to give more than she wanted to. The thought of someone pushing her past her comfort enrages him a bit.

She should be picky about who touches her. No one deserves her, not even him. He especially doesn't deserve her innocence. As willing, as he is to let her explore, he won't let it get too far. She deserves someone who can give her all the time and attention she deserves. Not a man who's going to neglect her to focus on school. He wants to make his parents proud and become a doctor. They would be proud of him no matter his chosen career path. He's the one pushing himself in this direction. They had informed him they will support his dreams.

Savannah is beyond excited about the progress the calf is making under their care. Kate told them earlier if he survives, she and Thomas can decide on a name for him. But, to not discuss it until he's well and truly out of the woods. She has been keeping the list of names to herself. Hoping to convince Thomas to pick a warrior name for their little fighter.

Thomas has been attentive all day. It's nice but different. Wondering if he thinks this morning was a mistake and he's trying to overcompensate for the letdown she's sure to receive. Trying very hard not to overthink everything, she's having little success. Even when she's putting most of her effort into the calf, there's still part of her that can't stop thinking about him. This morning meant so much more for her than it did for him.

"Do you want to keep him in my apartment again tonight?" She asks while feeding the calf.

"Yeah. I put extra clothes in my car in case that was your plan again," he shares.

"My plan? It needs to be a mutual decision," she cuts in with a little bit of irritation in her voice.

"Wrong word. I should've used suggestion instead of plan. I think it's a great suggestion," he corrects while she eyes him cautiously.

"How's it going?" Kate asks loudly to ensure they know of her arrival as she walks through the barn door towards the first stall. She overheard what appears to have been, an argument.

"Good, he's almost done with dinner," Savannah answers cheerfully.

"Planning another slumber party?" Kate teases. Thomas eyes her from where he's at.

"You think it's crazy, don't you?" Savannah asks dejectedly.

"Not at all. It's exactly what I did with Duke when he came to me. Although I'm jealous that you have the help, I wished I had. Raising two children and a newborn calf at the same time was exhausting," Kate explains. "Have fun. Let me know if you need help with anything."

As her aunt walks away, Savannah eyes Thomas who was watching Kate throughout the exchange. "He's done. Shall we take him to the pasture to go to the bathroom before he goes to bed?"

"After you," he replies with a gesture of his hands.

Another quick questionable glance at Thomas on their way out with the calf. Why is he being so amenable? Is staying the night going to ruin the friendship they are developing? Can she call it a friendship even though she touched his penis?

The calf is safely in bed, Savannah is showered and dressed, and Thomas is currently showering. She spent all day thinking about what happened this morning and what could have happened. Wishing they weren't interrupted so she could have found out. He emerges from the bathroom shirtless and in another pair of sweatpants. This time they're his own but still sitting rather low at his waist. The sight of it makes her ache between her legs. She knows what's a few inches lower and she wants very much to continue her exploration.

"Not a fan of my pants?" She teases with a wink. He does look more comfortable with his own.

"I have more room to grow in these," he answers with a wink in return.

"It grows more?" She asks with wide eyes, "how is that even possible?" Thomas barks loudly with laughter. "Shhhh, you're going to wake him," she scolds.

"He'll be just fine," he assures through his laughter.

They are back to teasing each other, that's a good sign. As they both get into bed, she asks, "did the events of this morning bother you? You were different today."

He stills. "Bother me? No. It gave me things to think about."

"Think about what?" She presses even though she's terrified his response will suggest they put an end to what happened this morning.

"You. All the things I can't believe you haven't experienced. Things I could teach you if you were mine," he answers with more honesty than he probably should have.

"Teach me anyways. I know I'm not your type, I already accepted that after the campfire. I won't expect anything more," she encourages while looking everywhere but directly at him.

He was busy tightening his drawstring while she was talking. The moment she said she wasn't his type he stopped fidgeting with the string. Whipping his head to look at her, he asks, "who says you aren't my type?"

"Not in so many words. Your actions said a lot more," she explains while now looking into her lap.

"When I thought you were messing with me like a toy? I don't appreciate being used in a game," he explains with irritation.

"Oh," she says weakly while sinking into the bed and feeling like a fool. She couldn't come up with a better response.

Getting into the bed next to her, "I like this genuine version of you. Not the version I saw when you were angry at the world. This Savannah is nice, approachable, and attractive. Your smile is back and I need to find ways to make you laugh. Listening to you while you were with your cousins at the campfire was musical," he explains while pulling her onto his lap.

She is more than a willing participant to be on this lap. Instinctually straddling him, she wiggles to get comfy.

"Savannah," he groans, "be careful with your wiggling." This girl has no idea what her indirect actions do to him. The thoughts that race through his head wouldn't prove he's a gentleman.

She wants to ask why, but then she feels it. "This doesn't feel like you're in control," she teases while wiggling her hips again. Wondering where it'll lead if she continues to torment him.

"I'm always in control, even now. My cock getting hard doesn't say otherwise. It's similar to you getting wet when aroused. You turn me on, Savannah. Immensely," he explains while holding her hips in place. "What would you like to do? Remember, sleep is an option."

"I don't have to give all of me unless I choose to, correct?" Needing to have confirmation. The way she is feeling, she probably wouldn't stop him if he tried to bed her. Sitting in his lap makes her ache with need.

"You don't have to give anything you don't want to. Just because I permit you to touch me, doesn't mean I have yours," he explains. Unless she chooses to? I'm not taking her virginity. "There are plenty of things we can do without me taking your virginity."

"Can I kiss you?" She asks with a little courage.

"That's all you want?" He asks with interest.

"If I'm being honest, I don't know what I want. I've never done anything other than kiss someone. I know I enjoyed that. I never had the desire to learn when the rest of my friends did. I heard their stories, which seemed to be unpleasant experiences," she explains while looking into his eyes.

"I feel like these might be things you want to do with a guy you want. I'm all for letting you explore and teaching you certain things, but I don't want to be something you regret," he replies. He feels as if he might be taking advantage because he has the advantage. He wants to give her every option to opt out before she regrets him.

"I've never wanted this with anyone else, only you," she explains sheepishly while trying to escape his lap.

"Oh no you don't," he growls while he grabs ahold of her. Throwing her onto her back, he straddles her while pinning her hands above her head. Effortlessly combining both of her hands into one of his, he cups her cheek. Looking into her beautiful lavender eyes for affirmation, he finds it. The hunger of desire in her eyes. Growling as he leans forward to softly capture her mouth with his. The shock on her face from being thrown on the bed made him laugh on the inside. He begins to kiss her slowly until her lips become more pliable. Once she begins to kiss him back, a frenzy starts. No one could call her an unwilling participant.

Coming up for air, he looks at her. Her beautiful lips are now swollen from their kiss. Her face is questioning why he stopped. He begins to kiss up and down her neck. Nibbling now and again while he makes sure some part of his mouth never leaves her skin. Taking his tongue, he trails it along her collarbone to the edges of her shirt.

"Thomas, kiss me," she requests breathlessly. Working his way back up her neck, finally reaching her lips, he kisses her fiercely. "No, where you were, my boobs," asking between kisses.

"You sure?" He asks with hesitation.

She pulls back. "Is it weird that I asked? I figured it would feel nice," she explains sheepishly and lacking confidence with her words.

"I'll show you 'nice,'" he mutters as he works his way back down her neck. His free hand makes quick work of her shirt. He pulls it up until the tip of her nose and both eyes are covered and her arms are bound, leaving her delectable mouth free for his pleasure. Grabbing one boob gently and putting his mouth on it, he begins to flick her nipple with his tongue. She gasps loudly at the contact. She wraps her legs around his back to hold him in place since her arms are bound.

He then decides to suckle on her nipple. Nibbling every once in a while. Making her moan loudly. He lifts himself to cover up her moans with his mouth. "Shhhh, the neighbors are going to hear," he groans while pressing himself against her. Her legs are wrapped around him and spread so widely that it puts him in the perfect position to push himself into her. He reaches inside his pants and strokes himself so close to her that his knuckles are grazing up and down against the clothing at her entrance. He can't. A tease for both of them. Now, back to the breasts, he goes.

She had no idea this is what she was going to get when she asked him to kiss her there. No regret in her book. He is doing very naughty things with his mouth that she can't seem to get enough of. Her hands bound and her eyes blindfolded make everything more thrilling. She has to close her eyes and focus on the sensation. If it's that good on her boobs, how much better will it feel between her legs where she's aching for him? He got her hopes up when he was brushing himself against her. Now he's doing the same thing to her other boob and it's driving her crazy. She wants more. What though? "Thomas?"

"Hmm?" He replies with a mouth full of boob.

"Kiss me lower, please?" She asks breathlessly.

He stills, "your stomach?"

"Between my legs," she asks while still breathless.

He brings his mouth back to hers and kisses her deeply. Reaching into the shirt he pulls her hair while kissing her. Bringing his lips to her ear, he whispers, "no."

"It's clean, I took a shower," she says to try and make her case. "I'll even wipe up the stuff that's gathered if that's what's bothering you?"

The image of her being so wet she feels the need to wipe herself up, makes his cock strain even more for her. Fuck! "First of all, you should never have to wipe yourself up before someone goes down on you," he explains while gripping the sheet up his knuckles turns white. It's killing him to not feel what he's done to her. "Second of all, and most importantly, it's too much for one night. You'll just keep asking for more until you beg me to slide inside of you. That I will not do," he explains. Letting her arms go and pulling her shirt down, he lays on his side of the bed. Patting the spot next to him with his hands, he says, "come cuddle."

"How can I cuddle after being rejected?" She asks while covering herself.

"I'm not rejecting you. I'm simply respecting you. Sometimes people get so caught up in their passion that they go farther than they intend. I don't want you to ever regret what we're doing," he explains softly. "If you were seasoned, I'd be all for it. You're not even mine. I don't have the right to take certain things you offer. Now, please come here."

Without saying a word, she slides into a cuddle. Head on his shoulder and her arm around his chest. Hoping the tears don't roll down her cheek and touch his skin. She promised herself she wouldn't put herself in a position to be rejected by him again. Everything with him feels so right, that she continues down the path that feeds her soul.

Using his fingers to lift her chin towards him to kiss her, he stops with concern, "why are you crying?"

"I'm tired of being treated like a child. But don't worry, I'll be fine," she says while rolling onto her other side away from him. She's had to pick herself up from the ground more times than she'd care to admit. After years of practice, she's mastered being able to cry silently with none the wiser. The skill it requires to breathe quietly while suffering internally isn't something she should pride herself on, but she does. Using her pillow instead of his arm, she begins to pour out her tears. She'll have to lay her cheek on a pillow soaked with tears, but it's better than letting him in. Better than allowing herself to be more vulnerable toward him. He can't hoard information over her if he's not privy to the knowledge.

He sighs loudly. He doesn't think she's a child, but he still doesn't think she's thinking things through. Turning to his side to spoon her, he gives her a kiss on the back of her head, "goodnight, Savannah." She's refusing to use his arm as a pillow, so he positions himself on his arm to be as close to her as he can.

"Goodnight," she returns with the even breath she's perfected. She's had many nights where her dad would catch her in bed at an early hour. Feigning exhaustion from the day rather than the emotional toll. Weakness is not something her father tolerates.

Chapter Fifteen

"What is the problem, Savannah?" Thomas asks with irritation. She's been snapping at him all morning

"Nothing," Savannah bites off. She slept terribly, yet again. No nightmares to keep her awake this time, just sadness.

"You've been acting weird since we woke up. Something is most assuredly off," he bites back. He wants to call her out on it. He knows she's still upset about last night. Why can't she understand he's trying to do the right thing?

"I'm in my head. No, I don't want to talk about it," she says with attitude. He probably doesn't understand rejection. The way he walks around while exuding confidence.

"I'm going to take the calf to the pasture. I'm sure Kate has put Duke away by now," he informs while trying to ignore her attitude.

"I think I'll stay here. I need a minute to myself," she replies with a turn in the other direction. She can't even look at him right now. It's taken a lot of energy to be mad at him. She would rather be kissing him, but he ruined it. Out of the corner of her eye, Thomas gives a hard look before he turns and walks away with the calf on a lead. She decides she would like nothing more than to find the elusive bison everyone keeps talking about. She's never needed to go to that side of the farm, which is why she has never been. Never had the desire to do so. She's seen pictures of them and doesn't understand her aunt's fascination for them. They're beastly creatures. She needs a bit of distance away from him and the distraction he brings with his proximity. All she keeps thinking about is the amazing attention he paid to her breast, then her thoughts jump to the rejection. Shaking her head to admonish herself before finally stomping off.

Finding the bison pasture, she notices two men off in the distance. Looking a bit closer, she finds it's the two idiots that cornered her at the feed store. Why would they be here on Kate's property? They don't work for her anymore. She said they never would again. The closer she gets to them, the more she realizes there are two calves enclosed on the loading dock and the idiots are trying to coax them into the trailer. They're stealing them! The poor babies are crying out for their parents. The parents on the other side are furious. Stomping and ramming into the gate. Such powerful creatures are no match for the fencing they've designed to enclose them.

She knows she has to free them, but how? She looks around to find where the latch is. The two idiots haven't noticed her yet. Too focused on the babies, they've neglected to watch their surroundings. What a dumb thing to do if they're trying to steal something. No one is on the lookout. Once she spots the latch, she runs up to it and releases it. The parents swarm into the enclosure and scare the idiots away from the fence.

Then, they notice her. The taller one, whom Savannah can't remember the name of, which is why she refers to them as idiots, grabs her. She fights to be let go, but he continues to hold her even tighter. The shorter one grabs a rope off of the truck and begins to bind her wrist. Once they've done that, they bind her legs. All the while she is screaming, "let me go, you idiots!" The taller one wraps his hands around her mouth to silence her. Even though his hands are filthy, she bites down and doesn't let go. One punch from whoever hit her is the last thing she remembers.

Thomas notices that Savannah has been gone for too long. It's not like her to miss a feeding, let alone two of them. He calls Kate and asks if she's seen her. Once she declines, he enlists her, Noah, and Archer to help him find her. To focus and help the best he can, he encloses the calf in the stall so he can sleep off the bottle he was just fed.

They search for over an hour until Kate notices tire tracks and the tampered fence at the small bison enclosure. Kate calls her friend to find out if he or his men had been at the site today. He insists no one has been there for a few days and asks if there's anything wrong with his bison. She assures him the bison are fine, but he needs to send someone out to repair the fence.

Calling the other three over, she shows them the tracks. "Have you been here?" Kate tries to ask as calmly as possible. Once the three of them decline, she starts to pace. Hopefully, no one has kidnapped her. Who would do that? Only a handful of people even know she's here. Would she have called a friend to come to pick her up?

After talking to the cops, she becomes irate. "They won't do a fucking thing unless it's been over 24 hours!" She yells at the phone she just threw to the ground.

"Babe, we'll find her. What did Dylan say?" Noah asks.

"He hasn't heard from her since I picked her up. That he just wrote it off to her being mad at his decision," Kate snaps. Eyes widening at her attitude towards him, she instantly says, "I'm sorry."

Instead of snapping back, Noah just grabs her and pulls her into a hug. Even with her denial that she doesn't need one, he continues to hold her. Finally, she melts and starts to cry.

"We'll find her, kid," Archer vows.

"Noah and I can drive around a bit to look for anything weird. We'll ask around to see if she stopped by to get some food or whatever. We won't bring up the fact that someone might have taken her," Thomas assures. "I hope we find her pissed off enough to walk around town instead of coming back." Coming back to him is what he wanted to say. Pissed off is something he can handle. A kidnapping, he won't be able to sleep until she's safely at home. "You and Archer stay here in case she comes back. Maybe the tracks and her disappearance aren't related," he says without conviction.

A few hours later…….

As Noah and Thomas pull up to the house, Kate walks out of the front door. Looking in the truck, there's no Savannah. "You didn't find her?" She asks with worry.

"No, I was hoping she was back at home and you were still yelling at her and couldn't call us," Noah answers.

Thomas paces the length of Kate's truck. Who could have kidnapped her? Who is stupid enough to mess with an ex-military man and his even scarier wife? Noah might've served, but he's seen what Kate can do when she puts her mind to it. The cougar she killed to save Noah's life is one example. He still can't believe she killed it with one shot from that distance. "I need to go check on the calf," Thomas butts into their conversation. He has no idea what they were saying since he was in his head. "I will stay at her apartment in case she returns in the middle of the night. She can kick me out if she comes home pissed at me. I just need to know she's safe," he says before he briskly walks away.

"Keep us informed. I don't care what time she returns," Kate shouts.

Without much of a response, Thomas raises his hand and gives her a thumbs-up. She will be missing a third feeding. Where is she?

Chapter Sixteen

It's been two days since she was taken. Two days of being beaten every time she resists, every time she says something they don't like, and every time she sticks up for herself. Beaten so bad that everything hurts. Every movement hurts. They've fed her minimal food and she's been tied up the whole time except for her bathroom breaks when they stand close enough by that she can't escape.

They have been arguing nonstop about how stupid it was to have taken her in the first place. They would have gotten more money had they just taken the calves if she hadn't gotten in the way. They fight over whose turn it is to feed her or take her to the bathroom. The only thing they don't fight about is whose turn it is to beat her. They seem to relish punishing her.

Savannah refuses to give in to their abuse. Refuses to let them break her. They'll have to kill her before she stops trying to fight for herself. They gag her when they go into town. It's very stupid of them to leave her alone in a tent bound and gagged. Each time they leave her alone, the span gets longer and longer. Neither of them wants to stay behind with her to ensure she doesn't escape. They don't think she can with her restraints. She tried and failed, but it leaves her plenty of time to think about her escape plan without the stress of them looming close.

Unfamiliar with the area, she doesn't know which way to go if she manages an escape. Following along the road would be a mistake. The woods where they're camping is dense, but not so much that she can't see through the trees in certain areas. No other signs of life have passed since they made it to this campsite they built.

They keep talking about ways to get ahold of Kate to exchange her for money. What idiots. What about Kate makes them think she has as much as they're asking? A million dollars? Nothing about her lifestyle hints that she has anywhere near that amount of money. Her house is barely even furnished. Her cousins don't have all the fun shiny things she had growing up. As far as she's aware, ranch owners don't make that kind of money. Kate always tells her that ranching is about passion.

If she can figure out how to untie the binds on her feet, she can manage an escape. She can run. Probably not very fast or very far, but she will try with everything she has to make the escape worth it. Anywhere is better than this smelly tent and the torture they inflict.

The familiar sound of tires has finally returned. Even as they step out of the vehicle, they argue about whose turn it is to feed her. "Let her feed herself this time. I'm tired of the bitch biting me," says the short one. She knows it's him without seeing him. She can distinguish their voices now. Although, she still can't seem to remember their names since their conversation never includes her. 'Hey,' is how they grab each other's attention.

With no gentleness from them, she's being pulled out of the tent. As they place her by the fire the short one unties the binds on her wrist. "If you attack me, you'll go back into the tent and starve," he says in anger. As she's being handed a sloppily made sandwich, she bites her tongue. It's not the worst thing they've tried to feed her. She begrudgingly eats it to give her the strength she's been lacking. Can't take advantage of an escape if she's too weak to even manage it.

After she's done eating the disgusting sandwich with meat that might be camouflaged as turkey, she pipes up, "I need to go to the bathroom." Of course, they argue over who takes her. The taller one loses.

While relieving herself, she notices her period has started. She's never been regular, so the bad timing doesn't surprise her. Thank you, you unfortunate mess. "I need a feminine product!"

"Why would I have one of those? Just use the toilet paper," the taller one yells back.

It doesn't surprise her that he thinks toilet paper would solve it. The two of them are unsightly. Filthy hair, raggedy clothes, and they have terrible breath. Why would they know anything about feminine hygiene if they can't even figure out their own? "That won't absorb it. It'll just make a bigger mess.

You don't want my bloody mess attracting animals, do you? That'll be fun for the carnivores!"

"Hold on!" The taller one yells while walking back up the hill.

She assumes he's walking back up the hill because she hears his footsteps retreating from behind her. She can make it a day or two without anything, but they don't need to know that. She's unbound, so it's time to make a run for it. Down the hill, running as fast as her weak legs can take her. She doesn't hear anyone chasing her just yet, but it won't be too long until he catches on. Legs aching from the bruises, she pushes on. If they catch her, they might be too mad to control their rage and she fears she'll end up dead. When they beat her last night, she was mentally begging for mercy. The pain was unbearable and after it was over, she stayed on the ground unable to move.

After running the entire length down the hill, she spots a familiar clearing that Kate took her shooting a few years ago. She can't run into the clearing or they'll find her for sure. Keeping along the trees and away from the road, she spots a tree that looks climbable. It's been years since she's partaken in that with her cousins, but she has to try. She can hear their yelling. Can't discern if they're coming in her direction and she doesn't want to risk looking back. Up she goes, which turns out surprisingly easy. The treetop above her is thick enough they won't be able to see her hiding amongst the branches. Once she's high enough that she can't see anything around or below her, she settles into the nook.

Once she stops rustling, she can hear their yelling. Not close enough to have heard her shift on the branch, but close enough that she's glad she climbed instead of continuing to run. Her weakened state wasn't allowing her to run as fast as she normally does. The sun is starting to set, which will help her conceal herself further. Now that she is sitting still, she notices the burning sensation in her ribs. The kicks they delivered yesterday are sure to be blamed for it.

As the sound of their arguing comes close enough, she closes her eyes. They're close, too close. She can't see, but they might be just under her tree. In fear of looking down, she closes her eyes. As children, we close our eyes because if I can't see you, then you can't see me. Since Savannah is not a child, she understands how silly that concept is. There is that feeling one gets when they're being watched. She's afraid of giving them that feeling or afraid of her eyes being seen through the tiniest of cracks.

Eventually, after much arguing, she hears their retreat in the direction of the camp. Instead of making the mistake and descending too early, she decides to wait. She'll give them an hour or two. The branch is only big enough for her to sit on, not big enough that'll she'll feel safe sleeping on it without falling to her possible death.

"Where is she?" Kate asks out of fear, "why haven't we heard anything from anyone?"

"The police say we need to wait patiently until we hear from the kidnappers. That they're doing everything they can to find them," Noah tries to comfort her.

"They're not doing their job if they haven't found anything," she begins to sob into his arms.

"We'll find her. Evidence has proven that she's tough like her aunt," he encourages while placing multiple kisses atop her head.

"I'm going out tomorrow to try and look for her. I'm tired of waiting impatiently while letting other people do what I need to be doing myself. No ransom, no nothing!" She shouts towards the end.

"Her dad hasn't said anything about someone reaching out to him? Or her trying to call home?" He asks with desperation.

"Ransom? Blackmail?" She asks herself aloud, then it clicks. "Those fucking idiots, I'm going to kill them!" She shouts in anger as she stomps in the direction of her phone. They've discussed ransom and blackmail multiple times. Why hadn't it clicked before now?

Looking at her strangely, Noah demands, "whom are we going to kill?"

"Those two idiots you beat up at the bar, Seth and Rusty. Savannah told me they cornered her at the feed store to relay a threat to me. I didn't think anything of it, until now," she explains while dialing the number for the police.

"You should've told me someone's threatening you," he admonishes with irritation. Not saying anything more when he notices her roll her eyes at his overprotective nature. Of course, those two idiots would be stupid enough to threaten her.

Walking far enough away from the road to steer clear of vehicles, Savannah figures the road will lead her to town. Which town? Hopefully, the one close enough to Kate's and will be rescued immediately. Every sound a tire makes on the road nearby makes her whip her head toward it and her heart races faster. She doesn't know where she's going. Terrified to approach any of the strange houses she passes in fear that she'll be unlucky and pick the one the idiots live in.

After another few hours of wandering, she spots a familiar house. Her pace has slowed significantly after the number of things she's tripped over in her search through the darkness. What are a few more cuts and bruises when she's already covered in them? The closer she gets to it, the more she begins to recognize the driveway she has walked along in the rain.

Approaching the back door to ensure she steers clear of the road, she softly and urgently knocks on it. Thomas has no dogs to alert him of her knocking. After a few tries of doing it softly, she begins to fiercely pound on the door. "Please be home!" She yells while looking around to make sure she wasn't followed.

The lights come on and an older gentleman approaches the door and slides it open. He looks like an older version of Thomas. The look of horror on his face tells Savannah just how badly she looks. Without words, she pushes past him and falls to the floor. She can hear him locking the door and closing the curtains. "Please tell me Thomas is here?" She chokes out as the tears begin to roll down her face.

"Thomas!" The man roars.

"Dad?" Thomas asks while rounding the corner. As soon as he sets eyes on her, he runs and scoops her up. "Call Kate and the police," he commands angrily. Hopefully, dad will understand the anger in his voice and won't take it personally. Carrying her to the sofa, he begins to take in more of her battered appearance. Black eyes, busted lips, cuts, and bruises along her arms and wrists. Her wrists look raw from rubbing against what he's going to assume was some sort of binding. She's in the same clothes he last saw her in, except now they're filthy and have tears in them. Savannah claws at him as she tries to climb even more into the safety of his arms. "Shhh, you're safe with me," he croons as he tries to hold her as delicately as possible. "Who did this to you?" He asks in a demanding voice even though he's trying not to scare her even more.

She can't stop crying. Violent shakes, uncontrollable tears, and a sense of terror that has captured her ability to speak.

Kate arrives at his house in record time. Foregoing proper shoes, she is in her pajamas and flip-flops. Noah is disheveled and barely had time to grab a shirt. He's barefoot. Kate would've left him at the house if he didn't get into the truck in time. She needed to see Savannah with her own eyes to know she was safe. She trusts Thomas implicitly, but no one can assure her more than her own eyes.

It's of no surprise that she beat the police to his house. They're a lot farther than the almost mile she sped through to get here. Letting herself into his house only to stop short. The sight of her niece with a bloodied and beaten appearance makes her see red. One look at Noah who also stopped short and she can tell he sees it as well. There's no saving whoever did this to Savannah. As she approaches her with a calm urgency, she sits next to them and asks with a trembling voice, "who did this?"

Savannah grabs ahold of her aunt and pulls herself onto her lap. Whispering with all her might, she croaks, "them."

One word and Kate knows. She knows she was right and she knows what she'll do if she ever sets her eyes on them again. Looking at Thomas and Noah, Kate says, "I was right, it was Seth and Rusty." Holding Savannah in a tight embrace, she whispers into her ear, "I'll make them pay for what they did to you."

Savannah nods as she continues to sob into the crook of her neck. Her violent shakes continue involuntarily. They make her body hurt with every movement and as the adrenaline subsides, she begins to notice her insides are starting to hurt as well. Like the kind of internal cramping your body gets when your body is too cold and it's trying to warm itself up with movement. As if Thomas could hear her thoughts, she hears him say, "I'll get you a blanket." Not being able to discern if she's cold enough for one, she'll take it for the comfort they also seem to provide.

The police and fire department get there within minutes of each other. The fire department examines her while she finally begins to tell her story to the officer. They are so tender and patient with her inability to bring out certain words.

"We have to bring her to the hospital. We need to make sure there's no internal damage," the fireman explains while next to the paramedic who finally shows up.

"I understand," Kate replies with a nod.

"No! I'm not going by myself! I refuse," Savannah shouts in anger.

Thomas scoops her up and carries her back to the couch. "I'm not leaving your side," he informs her with a gentle kiss on her head. "Let me just change my clothes," he whispers.

"Please don't leave me!" Savannah begs while clawing at his shirt again.

"Shhh, I'm here, I'll protect you," he croons. "Kate, will you get me clothes from my room to bring with me?" With a nod, she walks off in the direction of his room.

Walking into his bedroom, she notices how clean it is. She won't have an issue discerning which is clean or dirty. After grabbing a few outfits for Thomas, Kate also grabs sweatpants and a hoodie for Savannah to change into after they examine her at the hospital. Knowing Thomas, he won't be bothered by lending a pair of clothes until she can bring some later on.

Thomas rides with Savannah in the ambulance to the hospital. A ride that seems to have taken longer than it should have. Once in the hospital room, he stands to the side as the doctor and nurses begin to examine her. To give her a modicum amount of privacy, he averts his eyes as the nurses begin to undress her. After some coaxing on his part, he convinces Savannah to allow them to take her to run some tests. Promising that he'll be here waiting for her until she returns.

He spends the entire time she's gone for testing pacing back and forth. He's so angry. How can someone do that to another person? Why would they? The need to avenge Savannah brings his mind to terribly dark places. How would they feel getting the shit beat out of them? He doubts it would take much coaxing to have Noah join in on the fun. Would he be able to think straight and stop himself before he beat them to death?

Once she makes it back to the room, he allows the nurses to get her situated. As soon as they leave the room, he climbs into bed with her and holds her until she falls asleep. She was too afraid to close her eyes, so they decided to give her some medicine to help her rest better. "Your body heals best with rest," he whispers into her ear.

A nurse walks in while he lies there holding her in her sleep. "You can't sleep on the bed with her, it is not safe," she admonishes.

"There's no way you're separating us," he informs with a tone that suggests he's not to be messed with. With a roll of her eyes and a scoff at his attitude, she leaves the room. Two days of being worried and not knowing whether he'd ever see her again, shook him. Shook him so hard in fact, he realized then how much he cares for her. There's no way he's letting go of her now.

Chapter Seventeen

Kate woke up at 5:00 a.m. and dragged Noah out of bed to go with her. Even though they were up late, Noah was adamant that he didn't want her going without him. Archer spent the night on their couch so he can be there for the kids for protection. Kate wanted to go last night when they carted Savannah away, but Noah refused. Asked her what she expected to find in the dead of night. Other than listing the two idiots, she couldn't continue her argument.

It didn't take long to find the campsite Savannah described. Once she mentioned the clearing, she once took her shooting, Kate immediately thought of the closed campsite that's near there. It is closed because reckless idiots mistreated it. Judging by the sight of things now, the two idiots have not done any different. In their haste to leave, they left behind all their trash. There is nothing of note to help them find them. The fire is cold as ice, which means they didn't stay the night. They probably left once Savannah escaped.

Kate thought Savannah would get more sleep without everyone in her room, so she allowed Thomas to go without her. He's been filling her in on the details of Savannah's results. Dylan still refused to drive up here. Stated he would call her in the morning to check how she was doing. He can be a huge asshole. She cannot fathom reacting as he has if it were one of her own two kids. She would be doing the same thing for them as she has been for Savannah. Well, except she wouldn't allow them to spend the night in a hospital room without her.

Even though Kate was up without sleep for the two days Savannah was missing, she didn't sleep well last night. The details of the events Savannah shared only made her angrier. How dare they almost beat her to death? Kate has never wanted someone wiped from this earth, until now. The police are on a manhunt for Seth and Rusty. Now that they know whom they're looking for, they assured her they'll be found. She doesn't have much trust in the local sheriff's office to succeed in the task. She and Noah will be searching on their own when they have the chance. Her ranch still needs to be run, regardless of her thirst for blood.

With Savannah unable to and Thomas taking the lead in caring for her, Hazel is now taking care of the calf. She is enjoying it too much. Although, she might not have once it first got here. The calf can do more things on his own, so he's not constantly needing attention in the early mornings. Kate does the first feeding since sleeping beauty refuses to get up earlier than she normally does.

Thomas has informed her that Savannah needs to stay another night due to dehydration and to also ensure she doesn't have complications from her injuries. Savannah mentioned in her account of what happened that she had started her period. They did an ultrasound to check her for internal injuries since she didn't start as she thought. The doctor informed them that sometimes when the body undergoes trauma, blood may pass into the urine. They ran several tests which confirmed bruising on her ribs.

Thomas has refused to leave her side unless he is forced to. Still wearing the original clothing Kate had collected from his room. The nurse has offered to let him use a pair of scrubs if he is inclined to take a shower. Her tests pull her away from him more than he's comfortable with. The nurses help her when she needs to shower or change into a different hospital gown. He steps out of the room to give her the privacy she doesn't ask for. It's not his place to undress her here and she's not really of sound mind to consent while being on the pain medications they've given her for her injuries. He encourages her to take the help. That dealing with the pain because of pride would not be a wise choice.

After two days of being in the hospital, almost a third, she's finally back in her apartment. Kate can breathe a little easier now that she's home and she can help out and check on her when she's up for the company. She and Noah still haven't been able to find the men or any signs of them. They haven't been seen in town at all, so they probably know they're wanted.

She has a plethora of weapons at her disposal to use for the revenge she so desperately wants. Rifle, pistol, baton, and taser. She's skilled in all of them. Noah has been worried that her desire for revenge is taking away from her sleep. It has, but there's no helping it. She won't be able to sleep knowing they're still out there.

The first few steps into the apartment and Savannah is not sure what to do or how to act with Thomas. He was wonderful and attentive at the hospital, but they're not there any longer. Is he planning on going home now that she's back? Is his attention going to cease since she can have Kate and others help her if needed? So many questions running through her mind and she's terrified to ask. Afraid of receiving a devastating blow.

All of her clothes have been washed and neatly folded or hung in the meager closet. Kate must have cleaned. She probably wanted to make sure she came home to a comfortable setting. The doctor has ordered her to get as much rest as possible at home. Is this her home? During the short length of time that she's been here, it sure feels like it. Have things changed since she feels unsafe to even step outside? Would she feel safer back in the city at her dad's house? She doesn't know how much he would cater to her and her healing. Probably not in the least.

It hasn't even been a week since her rejection from Thomas to go further at her request. He said he was being respectful, but she didn't buy it. She's a grown-up who can make her own choices and deal with the consequences of them. Nevertheless, he's being a great friend and she hopes he'll continue to help her out as she needs it.

"No more nurses. I should probably call Kate to help me out of my clothes," she says aloud, but mainly to herself.

"I can help if you'd like?" He offers with a step toward her.

"Um, I don't know if that's a good idea. I think I might be able to manage by myself," she answers as she turns away. Slowly, she tries to pull her shirt over her head. Letting a small cry escape as she attempts.

"Stubborn woman, why won't you let me help you?" He demands as he begins to walk closer to her.

"Because I'm in a lot of pain," she bites off.

"Exactly, let me help you," he scoffs with a furrowed brow.

"No. I don't want to be in further pain," she bites off again.

"I'm not going to hurt you. I promise I'll be gentle," he returns as he takes offense.

"Emotional pain," she softly replies.

"Care to elucidate? I have no idea what you're talking about," he tries to speak gently and quell his annoyance.

"I can't handle any more rejection. I know you don't want me like that. You undressing me would be intimate," she trembles as she explains. Turning away from him again to avoid his eyes. If she sees his pity, she's sure to cry.

"I don't want you like that? Those must be some good drugs they gave you," he scoffs as he rolls his eyes while walking toward her. "If you're referring to the night I said I wouldn't eat you out, that was then. It wasn't rejection. I don't know how many times I can tell you I was respecting you before you believe me?" He explains while turning her around to look into her watery eyes, "please don't cry." Giving her a soft kiss on each eyelid. Slowly, he lifts her shirt starting with the hem, up and over her head while carefully avoiding any contact with her skin. Once it's completely off, he sucks in air through his teeth. Always giving her privacy, he never saw all the bruises and cuts she hid underneath her clothing. There are so many and it's becoming increasingly difficult to refrain from joining Kate's mission for revenge. Unhooking her bra to make her more comfortable while she sleeps, he spins her to ease the straps off of her shoulders and arms. Once he notices her avoiding direct eye contact, he whispers, "look at me, please."

She slowly shifts to look him in the eyes, only to watch him descend on her lips. Softly to ensure he doesn't worsen the cuts on her lips. "Are you taking pity on me?" She asks between kisses.

"I don't kiss people out of pity," he says as he begins to unbutton her pants. "When you were missing, I realized how much I wanted you. How much I need you around," he admits as he gets onto his knees. While he's kneeling, he helps her out of her pants and underwear. Savannah immediately covers herself with her arms and hands. Standing up, he moves them out of the way. "Don't ever feel ashamed in front of me. If you want me to stop, just say so," he whispers.

"Stop you from doing what?" She asks with wide eyes.

"I want to taste you. If you agree, get comfortable on your back," he orders.

She eyes him but does as she's told. Once on her back, her knees bend up and she covers her crotch with her hands. As much of her, as he's seen, she's still unsure of her body covered in all the wounds. They must look as unsightly as she feels.

He pulls off his shirt and jeans but leaves his underwear on. Carefully climbing into the bed, he pulls her legs straight and hovers over her. Holding himself up by his arms to not put pressure on her wounded body, he leans in to place a tender kiss on her lips. When he feels her try to deepen it, he pulls away. Trailing kisses down her neck, across her chest, and landing on her nipples.

She runs her fingers through his hair as he begins to nibble and suckle on her nipples and a soft moan escapes her lips. He's being so tender and she appreciates it. If she wasn't in so much pain, what would he be doing to her instead? "What are you doing?" She asks as he begins to kiss her tummy. The feel of his facial hair tickles. This unshaved version of him is her favorite.

Carefully passing her injured ribs, he begins to kiss her stomach and her hips. Making sure to get each side of her before he travels lower to her, "oh!" He hears her exclaim once he finds what he's looking for.

She's never had someone kiss her vagina before. It feels, interesting. Maybe because it's her first time, but she's very aware he's down there. "Thomas?"

He stills, "yes?"

"I don't know if I like this. I can't stop thinking about all the little details. I can't explain it, but it's different than when you were at my boobs," she explains while trying her hardest to not fidget with her hands. Where is she supposed to place them?

If she can form a clear thought, not to mention elucidate her thoughts, then he's not doing his job properly. "I can fix that," he replies with assertion.

Gently pulling her ass to the edge of the bed and getting on his knees, he throws one leg over each shoulder. Grabbing her thighs to hold her in place, he dives in. His tongue is on her clit flicking it up and down. Taking his lips, he begins to suck on her clit. Using two of his fingers to spread her lips apart while at work, he begins to lap up all the moisture flowing from her. She tastes incredible. So pure.

She would've jumped from his lips making contact if he wasn't holding her down. "Oh, wow," she breathlessly exclaims. Now this, she can get used to. All she can think about is never wanting him to stop. He's back to playing with her clit with his tongue, that's her favorite so far. "Oh," she squeals with delight when he adds a finger inside of her. On the occasion she's done this to herself, it's never felt as good as the way he's doing it now.

As her body begins to tighten up, she runs her fingers through his hair and pulls. Thomas must have taken it as the encouragement she meant it to be since his mouth is now working in overdrive. Tightening as much as she can, she begins to explode. Tiny contractions happening in all the best places. After a few moments, she finally relaxes every part of her body. He gets off his knees to lean in to kiss her atop her head.

"Hang on," he orders softly as he walks towards the bathroom to grab a hand towel and wets it under the faucet. After he wrung out the water, he walks back over to wipe her clean.

She just watches him. What else is she going to do? She's had no experience with things like this. Is this what every guy is supposed to do? She didn't hear this detail from her friends.

He walks back to the sink and places the hand towel on the counter. After he walks back to the bed, he lays on it. Grabbing her hand, he gently tugs to encourage her to come and lay next to him. Watching as she carefully moves into her spot next to him. Taking care to not cause further pain to her injuries. He can see she's in a lot of pain. Even with the pain medication, she still winces with each movement.

Leaning in for a kiss, he feels her begin to deepen it. Following suit, he also trails his hand softly down her body. Stopping between her legs, he uses his fingers to spread her lips as he begins to rub her clit. He uses two fingers to rub in a circular motion and a moan escapes her lips once more.

Pulling out of the kiss to look into her beautiful lavender eyes, he says with a husky voice, "don't you ever say that I'm rejecting you again. You have no idea how badly I want to slide my cock inside of you and make you mine. Slide it so far inside of you that you'll think I'm in your stomach. When you've healed enough that every movement doesn't require a second thought, I will make you feel things you've never imagined."

"Why can't we do that now?" She asks while panting. She can hardly form words while his fingers are providing so much pleasure.

"I can't fuck you how I want to while knowing you're in too much pain. The distraction will be too much. For now, I will take pleasure in giving you pleasure. Do you like this?" He asks even though he knows the answer.

"Yes," she pants. "Thomas!" She moans while grabbing hold of his pants for purchase as he quickens his fingers. After several minutes, the build-up becomes too much and she cries out as she shatters. He captures her mouth to muffle her sounds so their co-workers who live next door don't overhear.

With a last kiss on the top of her head, he covers her up with the blankets. Within minutes she's fast asleep. Medication along with satisfaction would make anyone succumb. Hopefully, she'll sleep through the night. The trauma she went through has been making it difficult for her to go to sleep and stay asleep. "Sleep well, my queen," he whispers into her ear.

Chapter Eighteen

"No," she softly moans, "stop."

"Hmmm?" He asks in a sleepy voice.

"No," she now repeats with a whimper.

Opening his eyes, he frantically looks around in the darkness, trying to find something that should not be there. Maybe a bug is biting her?

"Ow, please stop!" She begins to shout and thrash her head from side to side.

"What's wrong?" He asks urgently as he begins to run his hands along her body to check for something injuring her. There's nothing he can feel.

"NO! No, no, no. Leave me alone!" She shouts while hitting and kicking Thomas away from her.

He jumps out of bed to run and turn on the light. Noticing nothing around the room or near her, he looks at her face. Her eyes are closed, her face showing anguish, and tears are now beginning to leak out from her eyelids. Walking towards the bed, he softly says, "it's alright."

"Don't touch me!" She shouts once more while flailing her arms and legs.

Almost getting hit in the face, he decides to pin her down to prevent her from hurting herself. That was a mistake. "Ow, you're hurting me," she begins to cry out. Fearing he might be truly hurting her, he releases his hold. "Savannah," he says in a loud demanding voice in an attempt to wake her.

"Go jump off of a cliff!" She says with tears streaming like a river out of her still-closed eyelids.

He's had enough. He can't bear to see her like this any longer. She needs to wake up. "Savannah, wake up!" He begins to shout. Grabbing both of her shoulders, he begins to shake her awake. Her eyelids are thrown open with a look of terror in them. No words emerge from her. It must have taken several minutes of her staring at him like he was the bad man with her body as stiff as a board. "Savannah, it's me, Thomas. You're safe now," he croons with sadness without touching her. He has no idea how he'd feel if she recoiled from his touch. He has a very deep desire to never find out. "Savannah?" He watches as she starts blinking back to reality.

All she heard was her name coming out of his mouth. The immense pain in his voice. Why? Why does he sound like he's in pain? Shaking her head, she then begins to look around the room. "Thomas? What's wrong?" He looks as if he's afraid to touch her. Edging away from her as if her skin will set him afire.

"Savannah? Are you awake?" Asking with hesitation.

"Yes," she drawls with confusion on her face, "why?"

"You had a nightmare. A very violent one," he explains with sadness in his voice.

His words now explain the sadness in his eyes, the crease between his brows, and the crack in his voice. Eyes widen with a gasp. "Oh, no. I didn't hurt you, did I?" Please don't leave me now, I need you. That's what she wishes she dared to say aloud. She hates seeing him like this. She never wants to cause him pain.

"I'll be fine. Are you okay?" He asks while slowly reaching for her.

"I don't remember my dream. As far as I'm aware, I'm okay," she explains as she begins to look over her body. So far only the same cuts and bruises from the kidnapping. She lifts the covers to check that her lower half is fine as well. Then begins to blush as she remembers why she's naked. Glancing over at the clock, it's only 10:00 p.m. She's only been asleep for an hour? If that. She doesn't remember exactly when she fell asleep. Only the satisfaction made her sleep incredibly well. Or so she thought. Maybe she can pretend to brush it off to get him back into bed? "Come back to bed. I'm sorry I woke you up," she says tenderly while patting next to herself.

"I won't be able to sleep after that. You scared me. You sounded as if you were in so much pain. Yelling for me to stop," he explains as he begins to pace.

"Oh. I can take a guess as to what my nightmare was about. It's weird that I can't remember it," she says while trying not to scare him away. Will he continue to stay if these night terrors persist? Will this be the final straw to him leaving? He's already put up with so much. There's only so much one can take before they pull themselves out of the equation.

"How can you be so calm? Your cheeks are still wet from your tears," he asks with disbelief.

"I can't control my dreams. Everything scares me lately. I'm trying very hard to keep it together. Please get back in bed," she begs.

Picking up his phone as he walks over to the light switch, he flips it off. Heading back to bed, he's very aware of her eyes on him, even in the dark. Once he's under the covers, he pulls her close to him. He'll wait until she's asleep before he sends Kate a message informing her of what transpired.

"Thomas?" She asks meekly.

"Yeah?" He returns with a turn of his head to face her, even through the darkness.

"Please don't give up on me," she begs with sadness in her voice.

"You couldn't scare me away even if you tried," he reassures with a kiss on her head and an even tighter embrace.

It takes several hours for both of them to fall asleep. Neither one said another word as they lay there in each other's arms. Exhaustion took hold of him. Once he felt the heaviness of her head that assured him she was asleep, he couldn't fight it any longer.

Chapter Nineteen

"How serious do you plan on getting with her?" Archer asks while jutting his chin towards Savannah who's in the pasture with the calf.

"I don't entirely know how serious she wants to get. She's been through a lot and the last thing I want to be is a bad decision she makes while hurting. She's so much more than anyone sees," Thomas answers while watching her brush the calf. The baby has flourished and spends a lot of time in the pasture with the other calves.

"I've already known this about her. Kid, what do you want?" Archer asks quietly but directly.

"Her," Thomas admits.

"Just don't break her heart. She's been through enough in life," Archer warns.

"If anything, she's more likely to break mine. I've never wanted to be everything to someone. She's changed that," Thomas says with a smile towards Savannah as she begins walking with the calf towards them. "It took almost losing her to wake my ass up."

"Sometimes, that's how life teaches us the important lessons," Archer whispers to Thomas.

"Can you believe how big he's gotten?" Savannah asks the both of them as she closes the distance.

"I can't believe he lets you walk him without a lead. Reminds me of Duke and Kate. Except this one hasn't tried to murder us, yet," Archer laughs.

"He remembers what you did for him when he first got here. Now you understand why the goats follow Christian. He loves you," Thomas says with a smile.

Savannah looks at the calf who is using her as a leaning post. Even though the pressure from him hurts the wounds that are trying to heal, she wouldn't dare move him. He's too damn cute. "Do you honestly think so?"

"Absolutely," he responds after watching her eyes light up after his comment. He wants to keep that smile on her face. "Archer needs me to help him with his driveway. Do you want to stay here with the baby or come with us?" Thomas offers her the choice since he can still see the pain on her face as she walks.

"If I come, can I help?" Savannah asks.

Just before Thomas was going to tell her she couldn't help, Archer piped up, "Of course, kid. I'd appreciate the extra hands." As Savannah walks away to lead the calf back to the other cattle, Thomas whispers, "she's still in a lot of pain. Do you think letting her help is a good idea?"

"If you lock her in a bubble, she will resent you for it. I'm sure you can think of something she can do. Teach her how to use the box blade," Archer suggests.

As Thomas watches her trudge back up the hill, he agrees with a nod.

"Ready, kid?" Archer asks her.

"Yes," she says while panting from the exertion. When they reach Archer's driveway, Savannah finds a pile of 2x4s to sit on. The walk to Archer's shouldn't have been so exhausting, but it was for her. Her injuries exhaust her quickly and are rather painful. Especially the injury to her ribs. She knows she should have stayed behind, but she needs to feel needed. She wants to be involved in helping Archer build his life here. He's the only one who truly listens when she's having a hard time with her dad.

Thomas walks over and sits next to her. "Take as much time as you need to catch your breath. It's only been 3 days since you returned home from the hospital. Don't make me worry about you overexerting yourself," he says as he turns her chin towards his face to kiss her. Soft and tender. He knows she's in pain and won't admit it. As he pulls back, he sees a big smile on her face. "I'm going to help Archer set up the tractor, I'll be back," he says with a kiss on the top of her head before he walks off.

It takes them ten minutes to finish setting it up. Returning to Savannah with an extended hand, "ready to drive it?" He asks with a chin jut to the tractor. Archer is correct. He needs to find ways she can help without causing herself further pain.

Savannah's mouth opens wide in surprise. "Really?" She squeals.

"Yeah, I'll teach you," Thomas returns with a smile as he leads her to the tractor. He gets in and sits with his legs spread open. Lending a hand to assist, he guides her up the steps. "Sit between my legs." The seat isn't big enough for two normal-sized people, but she's small enough to fit.

"Hey! No funny business in the tractor. Keep it professional!" Archer teases.

She laughs at the notion. It's not even fully enclosed. What could they do in here that others won't see?

"I wasn't thinking naughty thoughts until he said I couldn't," Thomas whispers into her ear.

While Thomas begins to show her how to operate, she runs her hands along his legs until she reaches behind her back. "Savannah," she hears him warn. Continuing with her mission, she begins to rub his cock from the outside of his pants. Feeling that he's nice and hard, she begins to move her hips.

He grabs her lower stomach to still her. "The things I would be doing to you if I could. Pay attention and stop teasing. I don't need Archer kicking my ass."

She snorts, "can he kick your ass?"

"I wouldn't swing at him. If he wants to kick my ass, it's probably well deserved," he says into her ear. Turning on the tractor, he yells, "watch me for a bit, then you'll do the rest."

She nods as she watches closely. Once she takes over, she shouts, "this is so fun!" She's never driven a tractor before, never wanted to do so. Now, she wants to learn how to run all of the equipment. Controlling something this powerful excites her.

"You're a natural!" He yells over the noise. Once she is halfway done with the driveway, he decides it's time for payback. Holding her lower stomach in place, he slips his other hand into her pants. Watching as her head whips around to look at him, he returns with a devious smile. "Pay attention to the driveway," he warns, "Archer won't be happy if it's crooked."

It takes all of her to try and maintain focus on the road as he's doing wicked things with his fingers. Trying to wiggle to tease him back, she fails. He has a very strong hand holding her in place. She's never won against his strength. It thrills her more to know how strong he is compared to her. There are probably all sorts of wonderful things he can teach her in the bedroom with that strength. Reaching closer and closer to her peak, "Thomas," she moans softly. Just as she is about to explode, he pulls his hand away. "What the?" She protests. With a jut of his chin to the right of them is when she notices it, Kate and Noah walking straight toward them. He helps her put the tractor in park and turns it off.

"Look at you!" Kate beams. "I hate driving the tractor in the afternoon, it makes me flush as well."

"Thomas is a good teacher. You're doing a good job," Noah praises.

Thomas just smiles. He is a great teacher. He just doesn't think they'd be praising him if they saw what he was just doing to her before they walked up. Or the things he's been more than happy to teach her in her apartment.

"Thanks, this is fun. I'm happy to be contributing again," Savannah adds. The other part is more fun, but she won't bring that up in front of her aunt. There's no way she's going to be able to finish before she finishes up the driveway. He better not think of starting his teasing again. She might have to find a way to tease him tonight as payback.

"Finish up and meet us at Archer's for lunch," Kate suggests.

"Yes, aunt Kate," Savannah says with a nod. Finish up? She can't. But she'll complete the driveway. Goodness, her mind has been in the gutter since she came to this farm. What is this man doing to her?

As Kate and Noah walk away toward Archer's house, Thomas lets out his laughter.

"Great. That was such as tease," she groans.

"It's just a preview for later," he whispers in her ear. "Now let's earn our lunch and finish the job before they suspect something."

Later that night…….

As they walk into Savannah's apartment with Thomas leading the way just as he's done since she got home from the hospital, Savannah begins to undress once she closes the door. He continues to walk toward the bathroom to check and make sure no one is hiding in her apartment. He's done it every night since they returned home from the hospital to make sure someone hasn't snuck inside. By the time he turns to say something, she is standing there in just her underwear. Starting up a conversation as if nothing is out of the ordinary, "what did you want to watch tonight?"

"You," he says with a raspy voice. Nothing on, except her underwear. Her tiny, tiny underwear. Lifting his eyes to her breasts, he can tell she's a bit cold. Nipples are standing at attention as if waiting for his mouth to warm them up.

She laughs, "no, silly. On the television." After a few minutes of him just staring at her like he's a lion ready to devour its meal, she adds, "I guess I'll pick."

"You can choose whatever you want. I won't be paying attention to the television with you wearing next to nothing," he continues to struggle with his words.

"I know what I'd like to watch. Wanna take a guess?" She asks with a sultry voice.

"Couldn't tell you," he answers while never taking his perusal away from her length.

"You. I want to watch you touch yourself. I want to know what to do. What pleases you," she explains with a smile.

"Your touch does more to me than my own ever will. I just go through the motions when I'm alone," he answers while taking a few steps toward her. He doesn't want to touch himself. He wants to taste her.

Savannah darts around him and sits on the bed in her spot. Then she smiles, "come show me. I can't do much, but I can watch you. I have a feeling that watching you will please me."

As he walks toward her, he begins to unbutton his pants, and they start to fall with each step. Kicking out of his pants, he pulls his shirt up and over his head. It's her turn to have a shameless perusal of his gorgeous body. Well-defined abs, bulky arms, and muscular thighs for days. How does he find time to look like that? She's with him for most of the day except for when he goes home to have dinner with his parents while she dines with her family. Since the hospital, she's made sure to be with someone at all times.

As he sits on the bed, Thomas is unsure. He's never been asked to perform for another person. Not stage shy in the least, it's just weird. As he gets into a comfortable sitting position so she can watch, he leans over for a kiss. He needs her touch to get himself started. Kissing her tenderly to not reopen the cut on her lip as they did the first night she got home. She didn't complain, but he could tell she was being extra careful with it in the morning. Scolding him every time he made her laugh.

Leaning back against the pillows, he pulls himself out of his underwear with one hand and watches her begin to watch him. The interest in her eyes pleases him. As he strokes himself, he can tell she's aroused by the shifting in her seat. Moving his one free hand to place on her breast and rub her nipple with his thumb. Touching her increases the sensation of what he's doing much more than just looking at her.

It didn't take long for him to find his release in his hand. The disappointment on her face leaves him questioning what just happened. "What's wrong?"

"I thought there'd be more to it than that. It didn't last very long," she explains.

"What every man wants to hear," he laughs.

"Oh! That's not what I meant!" She blushes and adds a playful slap on his arm.

"I'm just teasing you. I told you I just go through the motions. I know exactly what to do to get the job done for myself and it doesn't take long. Touching you was a bonus perk. When I can finally make you mine, THAT, I will make sure to take my time. That, I will enjoy immensely more than my own hands," he explains.

"I'm sorry my injuries are postponing that," she says softly.

"Never apologize for not being able to have sex. Intimacy comes in more forms than just naked bodies. You don't owe me anything, ever," he says softly as he looks into her eyes with his clean hand pulling her head close to his. Going in for the final distance, he kisses her gently. "Not to be cheesy, but you're worth waiting for." Turning his body, he picks up a tissue to wipe his other hand clean.

With a roll of her eyes, she leans back and places a smile on her face. "I think you still need to make up for the tease on the tractor. I ache in different places now."

"At your service!" He jumps up and hovers over her perfectly. The look of fear in her eyes gave her away. "You thought I was going to land on you?" He asks with a chuckle. She nods her head. With a quick kiss on her lips, he begins to trail them to the spot between her legs.

"Never stop," she moans.

Chapter Twenty

Kate is a bit late making her rounds this morning since she felt the need to check up on Savannah. Thomas informed her that she has not been sleeping through the night due to nightmares. He is now making sure she takes her sleep medication.

It's been two weeks since Savannah turned up at Thomas' house. Two weeks of not finding the assholes who did this to her niece. Two weeks of frustration and disappointment. Kate is displeased, to say the least. The more time goes by, the more time she has to plan scenarios out in her head. She can't murder them, right?

Every day she carries her pistol, taser, and her extendable baton. Is it too much? Maybe. Noah sure thinks so. He keeps insisting that she doesn't need to perform her duties while wearing all of that. That one would suffice. She does not agree with that assessment. What if she wants to choose the one she doesn't currently have on her? Such disappointment will occur.

How the hell can those two idiots evade them and the police this whole time? The police keep telling her there are no new leads. That they've probably left the state, possibly the country. There's something in her gut telling her they're a lot closer than anyone suspects. Another closed campsite for example? Maybe they're being hidden by someone in town?

Walking the outer perimeter, she smiles at the progress Archer has been making. She finally carved out half an acre for him to build a forever home. She had insisted on a whole acre, but he declined it. Said it was too much for just him.

She was very pleased with how quickly he accepted her offer. She enjoys having him here. Here on the property and most importantly her life. Archer has become more than her best friend over the years, he's family. She has never asked his opinion on them being family, but she's pretty sure he feels the same. She's never met his blood relatives. As far as she's aware, he doesn't even have a relationship with them.

The framework of his house is complete. His cute two-bedroom home is not grand, but he plans on adding all the bells and whistles city life would provide. Archer is a very tech-savvy person and wants his home to represent him as such. He has a private road to come and go as he pleases. An amazing view overlooking the bison pasture. He can build a porch to drink his coffee and watch their beauty. Well, that's her personal opinion. Archer doesn't think they're beautiful, he just thinks they're cool.

Wait, who's parked by the bison entrance? Squinting against the sun to get a better view. "Those sons of bitches!" She exclaims to the space next to her. Trying as hard as she can to have the element of surprise, she has to take the slightly longer way. Texting Noah on the way about whom she sees and where. Hopefully, she will get there before he does or he'll ruin her fun.

She's about fifteen feet away when she hears their incoherent arguing. Savannah had mentioned that they almost always argued during the kidnapping. With a roll of her eyes, she continues to creep toward them. Extendable baton in her hand and ready. Close enough to finally hear them clearly, she can decipher they're arguing over the new lock the owner had installed on his bison enclosure. She had forwarded the warning to the owner and he insisted on having someone put the best that money can buy. The bison are worth a pretty penny and he said it is worth the investment. Bolts so large it would take a mighty expensive tool to cut through them.

With a flick of her wrist and the click that ensures, she swings low. The sound of the now fully extended steel baton against the taller one's kneecap made a sickening cracking sound that she took too much pleasure in. Down he goes. Now, for short stuff. He starts coming towards her in an attempt to grab the baton from her, but she has other plans. Another swing, this time high to make contact with his forearm as he attempts to block her blow. Another, let's not lie this time, pleasurable cracking sound in the books. She quickly puts her baton away and pulls out the pistol. Taking turns to aim at each of them, "don't move, or I'll shoot."

The two men are holding their, from the way they're bent, broken bones. Crying out in pain, the taller one, Rusty, yells, "you crazy bitch!"

Kate laughs a little too hard while continuing to point the gun at them. "You shouldn't call someone crazy when they have a deadly weapon pointed at you. One little slip and whoopsie, dead! Of all the things I envisioned I'd do to you if I found you first, this happens to be the nicest. Feeding you to a pair of hungry hogs was another option, but it's wrong to starve the hogs just to torture you. Letting Duke have his way with you. I think he'd enjoy that. Especially if I was also in the pasture and he was under the impression that you were coming for me. He really is the best bull around. But then I thought about it and I wouldn't want someone in your family asking for him to be put down. That would never do. His life is worth far more than yours. Letting the bison tear you apart is another. I mean, we are right here. You have already fuddled the theft once. What's one more where you fall and slip inside the cage? They're very smart creatures. They remember the terrible thing you tried to do with their calves," she ends with a shrug. You think she'd be angry. She's past anger. She's focusing on everything to ensure they successfully leave in handcuffs.

Their eyes are incredibly wide at her suggestions. "You'd never get away with it," Rusty retorts.

"Maybe. Maybe not. We'll never know now, won't we? How's that knee feeling? We're pretty far from town and it takes them a while to get here. You'll have to sit in pain for a bit and think of how much easier you got off than you should've," she says with a light tone. She notices something out of the corner of her eye, so she snaps her attention to it. It happens to be Noah who is lazily leaning against the bison enclosure, observing. "Just here for the show?"

"Do you think I have a death wish? I'm not getting involved when a woman is out for blood. I'm just here as your witness," Noah winks.

Another movement catches Kate's eye and it's short stuff charging toward her. "Stop," she warns while taking a few steps back. No sign of slowing down, so she aims. With a deafening bang, short stuff falls to the ground. A single shot to the forehead is all it takes. There's no waking up from this one.

Noah knew the moment the shorter one was about to get up and attempt to disarm her. It took all of his willpower not to jump in and protect Kate. Someone might think less of him for not doing so, but this was her chance for revenge. Her chance to set things right for Savannah. Not that Savannah had ever asked Kate to do such a thing. She'll sleep better knowing one of the men who harmed her in such a way, is no longer walking the earth. Seth will never be able to harm her again. The amount of red he saw after seeing Savanah in Thomas' lap, was indescribable. Her bruised and beaten body from their torture still haunts him. He wanted to torture them himself.

Rusty hasn't attempted to get up and battle Kate. He might be the wiser of the two idiots. If such a thing truly exists? He just sits there with wide eyes. Frozen in shock about Kate following through with pulling the trigger.

The police and paramedics finally show up at the scene. Rusty went with a police escort to the hospital to get his knee taken care of. He'll always have the reminder of the day he messed with Kate. No amount of surgery will make his knee as it once was. Kate and Noah are questioned well into the night. The stand-your-ground law is what saves Kate from going to jail. Thankfully they live in an area that has such a law. The no trespassing signs, the attempted theft, the right to protect one's property, and the self-defense.

How is Savannah going to handle the news?

Chapter Twenty-One

"Are you okay, babe?" Noah asks with worry in his voice.

"Better than I probably should be. It would probably feel differently if it were vengeance for myself," Kate answers.

"Meaning?" He asks with a furrowing brow.

"Even with the trauma I've been through, I've never wanted revenge for myself in the way I wanted for Savannah. I wouldn't have shot him if he had stayed on the ground. I didn't enjoy that. Although, I did enjoy using the baton. I had to restrain myself from doing more damage. Is that wrong? It doesn't feel wrong to me," she explains.

"No, I don't think it is. If you were the one in Savannah's shoes, I wouldn't have stopped until they were both dead. I know you handled it better than I would have. When I watched him stir, I knew what he was going to do. When I gave you the wink, I knew what you were going to do in return," he answers.

"Do you think Savannah should stay in Hazel's room? She might feel safer," she asks with concern.

"She might feel safer? Or, will it make you feel better? I think Thomas is keeping her safe enough. They haven't spent a night apart since she returned," he chuckles.

"Yeah, I know. Maybe it is because I would feel better if she were under my roof," she admits.

"She's old enough to have a guy sleepover. Calm your mama bear down," he chuckles as he walks toward her.

"You trying to distract me with your presence?" She asks suspiciously with one brow raised.

Noah picks her up by the waist and lifts her onto the kitchen counter. "I would never dream of it," he returns as he begins to pull her dress up. "Whoopsie!" He exaggerates as he pulls her underwear to the side and begins to rub.

"Terrible liar," she admonishes while shaking her head.

Bending over to reach between her legs with his tongue, he licks just enough to make sure she's wet enough for him. Undoing his pants enough to accomplish his end goal. As he begins to pull away, he feels her grab his hair to hold him in place. Smiling against her, he grabs her wrist to release her hold as he stands up. He picks her up off the counter, sets her on her feet, turns her around, then bends her over. Pulling the panties down to her knees, he lifts her dress and slides himself into her. Pulling himself out, he asks, "did you want to finish our conversation?"

"Are you kidding me?" She demands. Just then, he slams himself back into her. "Noah!" She moans loudly.

Picking up the tempo, he pounds into her over and over. Making her forget her worries with the right kind of distraction. He grabs the back of her hair and pulls it to make her arch.

What conversation? She is so lost in the pleasure that she can't even think straight. Her eyes rolling to the back of her head and her toes curling type of pleasure. Noah has great stamina. After about five minutes of pounding into her, he switches from pulling her hair to wrapping his hand around her throat. Pulling her backward enough to kiss her deeply while still pounding into her. The sensation of being choked by him is her undoing. She explodes around his cock and he follows shortly after.

It's only been a day since it happened and Savannah still can't wrap her head around what Kate did. She killed someone in self-defense but killed nonetheless. The only thing she knows for certain is the envy she holds inside of her for not being allowed to do it herself. Morbid? Maybe. So much pain and terror fill her insides. Terrified to go anywhere without Thomas. The physical pain she still feels from her injuries. Emotional pain from the events. The terror that fills her dreams. Why has she gotten the shit end of the stick in life? First, the frat party. Now, the kidnapping. Is nowhere safe? Surely doesn't feel like it unless Thomas is there to protect her.

Other than fooling around, she and Thomas haven't verbally committed to being anything more than friends. It feels like a relationship to her, but it might all be in her head. If Savannah's being completely honest, she's afraid to even ask the question. If he rejects her, the situation would be too awkward for him to want to stay the night, or for her to even want him to stay the night. She needs him, wants him, and can't make it through the day without talking to him.

No, it's not fair to let him decide everything. She's not even sure if that's what this is. She's afraid in numerous ways. This route just seems less terrifying, for now. "I need to get out of this apartment or I'm going to lose my mind," she says out loud as she paces back and forth.

"I thought your ribs were hurting earlier?" He asks with concern in his voice.

"They do, but I need air. I feel like these walls are closing in on me. Can we go for a walk?" She asks while panting heavily.

"Sure, for a bit. If you get worse, I'm taking you to get checked out," he responds as he walks to the front door to open it for her.

Out the door, they go. She knows exactly why her feet are taking her in the direction of the bison enclosure. More specifically, to the crime scene. She's been itching to go and terrified to do it alone. Terrified to ask because he might say no and try to talk her out of it. She's been having difficulty breathing since she heard the news. Needing air wasn't a lie. She was having more difficulty breathing in her apartment with the walls surrounding her. She's been feeling as if her lungs are collapsing, but she hasn't said anything to anyone. Claiming it's her ribs instead, because who wouldn't believe her while they are bruised? She doesn't want to be admitted back to the hospital to be poked and prodded once more.

"Should we be here?" He asks once they reach the crime scene tape. He had a feeling she was leading him here. He was hoping she was just taking a weird route to Archer's.

"The walk felt like gravity, pulling my feet toward this spot. Not sure if we're allowed, nor do I care," she answers with a shrug. Walking around the tape and taking in the scene, she stops short of the sight of blood splattered across the fence. "Oh, wow. I didn't think I would see the blood," she says while trying to catch her breath. "Thomas, I can't breathe," she gasps while holding her chest.

"Hold on," he shouts as he pulls out his phone. He sets it on top of Savannah's chest and picks her up. Walking as quickly as he can without dropping her, he tells his phone to dial 911. As he reaches Kate's back porch, he gently sets her down on the floor. Still on the phone with 911, he throws the back door open and yells, "KATE!" As loudly as he can. Savannah is still breathing as far as he can tell, but she's still gasping. "Hold on, someone is coming."

Kate comes running out of the house with Noah in tow and takes in the sight. Dropping to her knees, she begins to check Savannah's vitals. "What happened?"

"She kept complaining about not being able to breathe," Thomas answers.

"Hold on, Savannah," Kate urges. It took ten minutes for the paramedics to arrive. "Took you long enough," she snaps.

"Kate, you live out in the country," the one paramedic bites back.

Noah reaches out and grabs Kate by the arm and begins to hold her back. "They can't help her if you beat them up," admonishing her attitude.

The ride in the ambulance seems to have taken forever for Thomas. Kate was fuming when the paramedics told her she wasn't allowed to ride with them. Even while Noah was holding her back, she kept yelling at them for not working fast enough. He might've been holding her back in fear of her being arrested. How do you think assaulting a first responder after killing someone in self-defense would look?

Thomas promised to keep them updated since they decided to stay behind. Kate needs to feed the kids dinner and Noah stayed behind to help her. Back to the hospital, they go. Maybe they'll just reserve a room on standby seeing as how they're making frequent trips?

Since she has remained conscious with the help of an oxygen mask, she permitted the doctors to share the details of her status with Thomas. The number of times he's accompanied her to the hospital, it's starting to feel normal for him to be this involved. He even keeps better track of her medication and habits. Whenever she gives the wrong information, he'll correct her. She chalks it up to him wanting to be a doctor.

Thomas has never been this involved with a female before. He usually bails at the first sign of complication. He's never wanted complications in life to deter him from his path to becoming a doctor. Now, he's sleeping next to her every night and worries about her throughout the day. He's always with her and still, he worries. He even knows that she's yet to have her period since she showed up at his back doorstep.

The only time he's away from her is when he goes home to have dinner with his parents. He'll work out, shower, and grabs fresh clothes to have at her house. Laundry is piling up in his room and the neglect is starting to leave a stench. His mom has offered, but he won't allow her to wash his clothes since they're his responsibility. Once his minimal obligations are finished, he rushes back to her. He's always been in control. He hasn't felt very in control lately.

While sitting quietly next to Savannah, the doctor walks in. With a finger to his lips as the universal sign of 'be quiet,' he slowly walks over to where the doctor is standing, which is at the far side of the room. "Any news?"

"She's had a panic attack," the doctor puts it simply.

"What could've caused it?" The more he knows, the better he can help her.

"With as much physical and emotional trauma as she's been through lately, a large number of things could have triggered it," the doctor answers.

As the doctor goes into more detail about panic attacks, Thomas's eyes remain on Savannah. Even in the safety of the hospital, he wants to hold her in his arms to keep her safe. "What is happening to me?" He asks himself just above a whisper.

Chapter Twenty-Two

The ride home thus far has been met with silence. All Savannah can think about is how much less she feels like an adult. Another prescription has been added and everyone is worrying over her even more. A panic attack, what's next? Plague? Loss of limb? All she wants to do is scream. She just might if one more person asks if she's okay. How can she attempt to get past this when everyone won't let her forget her back luck? When her traitorous mind won't settle down enough to heal. Kate has suggested she see a therapist. She doesn't want to go and doesn't need to talk her problems out with a stranger. She just wants everyone to stop treating her like an invalid. To stop treating her as if she will shatter.

Completely exhausted from the whole experience, all she wants is her bed. It's hard to sleep in a hospital. People come and go into the room to check on her, give her medicine, poke, prod, and take her for tests. It gets old, fast. They kept saying they wanted her to rest. Yet, they never actually allowed her the time to adequately do so. Once she gets home, she will try to sleep for a whole day, and Thomas can focus on work without worrying about her.

Once they pull into the driveway, she leaves the car without a word and begins walking to her apartment. "Savannah, where are you going?" Kate shouts.

"Home. I just want to go back to sleep," Savannah shouts without looking back. Two more minutes of walking and she'll be inside. A quick strip of her clothes and she'll be comfortable enough to fall asleep.

Thomas runs to catch up with her. "Hey, weren't you listening to your aunt? She wants to make us lunch," he says while grabbing her arm to pull her to a halt.

"I guess I wasn't. All I keep focusing on is how much I feel like an invalid. I'm tired and I just want to go to sleep. You can go about your day at work. I'll be in bed if you need to find me," she says with defeat in her voice. Eat? Food is the last thing she wants.

"Are you……" Thomas begins to say

"If anyone asks me one more time if I'm okay, I'm going to scream," Savannah interrupts. With that, she stomps off.

Thomas walks back over to Kate and explains the exchange he just had. Instead of staying for lunch, he decides to head to his own home. A good shower and a bed to himself sound like just the ticket after their hospital stay. So many bodies in and out of that room didn't give either of them a chance to rest. Poor Savannah.

The shower was nice and hot, but lonely without Savannah in there with him. No one to lather up makes a shower rather boring. How can he miss her? He's been with her non-stop. If he wasn't so unbelievably exhausted, sleep would've been unimaginable unless he was next to her.

By the time he wakes up, it's nighttime. He slept so hard that he woke up to a very wet pillow and drool soaking into his cheek. Gross. His aching body is what woke him. Aching to be near her. Aching to touch her. The more he begins to think about being next to her, the harder his cock becomes. Grabbing some fresh clothes, he gets into his car and begins to drive to her.

It only takes a few minutes with his swift driving. As he attempts to walk in, he finds the door locked. He begins knocking loudly with the determination to wake her. She doesn't have a spare key hidden, or else he would've let himself in to allow her to sleep longer.

Savannah is abruptly woken up by a pounding on her apartment door. "What in the world?" She says angrily. Getting out of bed, she walks over to the door to open it and finds Thomas with such determination on his face. She was sleeping so well before this rude interruption. For the first time in a while, she was able to sleep without taking an aid.

Without a hello, Thomas has her in his arms. "I need you," he hoarsely explains. Kicking the door shut, he begins to back her up to her bed. Kissing her fiercely the whole way.

Finding her with just a robe on makes it easier to accomplish his goal. He begins to frantically kiss all over her neck while squeezing her breast. Laying her down, he works his kisses from her neck to her breast. Taking one nipple at a time and devouring them in turns. He feels ravenous for her. Not taking a lot of time at her breast, he begins to work his way down between her legs and reaches her beautifully tight center.

He begins to feast on her as if his life depends on it. Licking, sucking, and nibbling her clit. Doing everything he knows to drive her crazy. Wanting her to reach such a pleasure that she will continue to flow her tasty flavor into his mouth. She tastes incredible. From the sound of the loud moans that are coming out of her, she's enjoying it almost as much as he is.

She has no idea what prompted this sudden need for her, but she's loving it. It doesn't take long before she explodes all over his mouth. With such an amazing release, she decides to stay in her languid position.

"Stay in that position. I want to look at you while I jack off. You're so beautiful, Savannah," he groans. Getting into position to sit next to her, he pulls his cock out of his pants. Moaning as it springs free.

Her eyes grow wide at the sight of him. "I've never seen you that big before," she says with her mouth gaping open. How is that supposed to fit inside her when she's healed? His cock might cause a new type of injury.

"You make me so hard and I need release. It's too painful to hold back," he explains while stroking himself.

Savannah gets up and spreads his legs into the letter V and settles herself in between. Sitting with her butt on her heel, she lightly runs her hand up his thighs. Using her right hand, she moves his away to replace it with hers. She begins stroking his massively hard cock with her small hand and makes him moan with pleasure. She can't help but think how much fun this is.

"Fuck, Savannah, that feels so good. It's taking everything I have to not fuck you right now. I want your tightness to swallow me whole. To drive myself so deep into you that you feel as if it's in your stomach. Maybe even in the back of your throat," he groans.

My throat? Now that's a good idea. She leans over, takes his head in her mouth, and begins to suck. Slowly taking more and more of him with each bob of her head. Testing the levels of pressure against his auditory reaction.

"Keep sucking harder," he encourages, "I'm almost there."

Savannah sucks even harder and goes a little further. There's no way it can all fit into her mouth. She still has no idea how she's even going to fit in between her legs.

"Get ready," he warns.

Get ready? What does that even mean? Now doesn't seem like the right time to stop and ask questions. She knows how upset she would be if she was almost there and he stopped to have a conversation. Could you imagine how much that would ruin it? What the……….

He effortlessly flips her onto her back and straddles her stomach. Grabbing his cock, he begins to pump fiercely. With loud moans, he begins to squirt himself all over her breasts. Dipping the head of his cock into the pool of semen, he shoves it back into her mouth. "How do I taste?"

She licks all around the head while he's in her mouth. Sucking to get a little more of a taste. When he pulls himself out of her mouth, she teases, "I could go for more." She really could. It doesn't taste bad like her friends all told her it would. Now she begins to wonder why the stories from her friends aren't even close to being similar to the experiences she's been able to share with him.

"I know we can make that happen," he says with amusement in his voice. Barely able to walk to the sink, he picks up a towel and wets it. Walking over to her, he cleans himself off her. Balling the towel, he chucks it into her laundry hamper. Score!

As they both lie there, exhausted after receiving their release, she pipes up, "how is it possible that you can fit all of that inside someone?" Not wanting to think of him with another girl, but she's becoming nervous.

Chuckling softly, "if done correctly, it's pleasurable for both. Are you worried I'll cause you pain?"

"I'm nervous it'll hurt. All of my friends talked about their first time and how they didn't exactly enjoy it. I'm beginning to understand why," she explains with her head on his chest while drawing imaginary lines on his muscles.

"I can't speak for the experiences your friends had, but I'd never push you to do something you didn't like. Have I hurt you thus far?" He asks while mimicking the tracing on her back.

"No," she responds immediately.

"We'll go at your pace. When you're healed, we'll discuss more of the details. Don't work yourself up over it. I promise you'll enjoy yourself even more than you do now. Let's order something to eat. We can drive into town and pick it up. If you'd rather, you can stay here naked in bed, and I'll go pick it up, he adds with a kiss to the top of her head. He hopes she won't stress herself out over this. He can't wait to have her legs wrapped around him. Can't wait until he can make her completely his.

Chapter Twenty-Three

It's been three weeks since her panic attack fiasco which led to her being hospitalized. Three weeks and she has finally gotten to the point where she can move without wincing. The first week back from the hospital was essentially bedrest. They did wonderful things in bed other than rest, but being confined in bed did not sit well with her. She couldn't bear it any longer. It took more convincing than it should have for him to let her leave the apartment.

She's been following Thomas around the farm for the last couple of weeks. Similar to a lost puppy. He wouldn't let her help with anything other than incredibly light stuff. A toddler would probably have had more responsibilities than her. He's been overprotective, to say the least. In truth, she doesn't mind. Even with complaints, she's enjoying that he cares so much for her well-being. There were a few nights she stayed at his house. His bed is not nearly as comfortable as hers, but she enjoyed something different. The walls of her apartment were starting to feel like a jail cell.

She laughed when he started doing his endless amounts of laundry. She's never known a guy to have so many clothes. He blames it on his mom buying him a new college wardrobe.

That she refused to let her son live in the city in his farm clothes. Why he doesn't do laundry at the farm when she does, she'll never understand.

His mother is very endearing. She's always full of smiles and has welcomed her into their home. While Thomas does laundry or whatever else he needs, his mother, Lana, pulls her to the side to show off their old family photos. She even showed Savannah a cute photo of Thomas naked in the bath. He must have been younger than five, but Lana said, "look at his cute tushy." When bringing up the topic later in bed, Thomas just laughed.

Just from the photographs, she can tell his childhood was much different than hers. A slight pang of jealousy hits her. She'll never know what it's like to grow up in a household with parents who are proud enough to show embarrassing pictures. Even in the photographs, she could see how loved he is.

The first night she slept in his room, she thought it would be awkward with his parents down the hall, but it wasn't. It might be because the two of them still haven't had sex. She was in too much pain before to contribute much of anything. A few things she could do, but Thomas informs her their carnal activities will hurt if she can't even do a simple thing such as bend over without wincing. The nights in his room are spent innocently cuddling until they both fall asleep.

The pleasure he's been giving her at her apartment has been impressive. She's never been able to please herself as well as he has. She can't stop thinking about how sex will feel compared to what he can do with his mouth and hands. She's eased up a bit with her concerns. They're still in the back of her mind, but his comfort makes her less nervous.

Before Thomas, sex was never on her mind. Now, the thought consumes her. She's heard horror stories from her group of friends and their first time. She's heard some great things as well, but the horror stories are what deterred her from amorous activities in the past. The pressure she used to receive from her ex-boyfriends also solidified it. She never wanted to give all of herself due to pressure.

That was then and this is now. She has so many questions she doesn't even know where to begin. Aunt Kate seems to have a healthy relationship with Noah, maybe she should ask her.

Thomas has no idea how much pain she's still in. He's asked, but she seems to play it off. His appetite for her is insatiable and he can't wait to finally have all of her. Every night he needs to taste and touch her just to feel some sort of satisfaction. His entire body aches to be inside of her. No matter how much he aches, he would never force himself on her. He knows she craves him also, but her pain deters him from trying. There is no way he'd be able to stay hard with pain showing in her eyes.

There have been a few nights where pleasing her had left him painfully hard and he had to relieve himself. She always wants to watch when he does. The fascination in her eyes amuses him. He's never had someone ask him to let them watch. Before Savannah, he could go months without feeling the need to pleasure himself. This constant need is new for him. She does something to his appetite and patience that he can't quite put a finger on.

"Aunt Kate, may I ask you something personal?" She asks while joining Kate for the walk around the perimeter.

"Anything," Kate answers with a shrug.

"How did you go about planning to have sex with uncle Noah?" She asks bluntly. She might as well just ask. No sense in beating around the bush when she wants straightforward answers.

Kate freezes. "How I planned it?" Oh, no. Has Dylan never given her the sex talk?

"Yes," she answers along with a nod.

Resuming their walk, Kate answers, "other than wearing matching bra and panties, it wasn't exactly planned. There was a bunch of built-up tension from being close to each other. When the opportunity presented itself, we both took it."

"Oh," she answers with a tone of disappointment. That's not the answer she was hoping for. She wanted more than a description of their spontaneity.

"Are you wanting that opportunity with Thomas?" Kate asks. Still unable to believe she's having this conversation with

Savannah. Also, thankful Hazel hasn't begun this line of questioning yet.

"I do. He said he's afraid he's going to hurt me because of my injuries," she acknowledges.

"That's very courteous of him. You can't find fault in him for that," Kate responds calmly. "Has your dad talked to you about being safe?"

"Yes. How do I let him know I'm ready?" She persists.

Taking a deep breath in to avoid the wrong reaction, Kate stops walking and turns to Savannah, "educating my niece on how to seduce a man isn't my strong suit. You'll still be that little girl in my mind no matter how much you now look like a woman. My advice is simple. Wear something you're confident in. Not what you think he'll like most. You can either be vocal about what you want or you can take the lead. If it's something he's also ready for, he'll join in. If he says no, you'll have to respect that." After a moment of silence, she adds, "I've seen how he treats and respects you. I know he likes you. Just remember, consent is a two-way street."

Opening her mouth to reply, she decides against it and shuts it for a few moments. "Thank you," she finally responds as they begin to walk again. Something she's confident in? That doesn't rule out anything. Thomas makes her feel confident in whatever she wears, even when she's wearing nothing at all. She still feels unsightly with the yellow bruises all over her body, but he doesn't remark upon them. He makes her feel as if they're not even there at all.

Kate sighs loudly. "Kid, just be careful. That's all I ask."

"I will," she replies softly. She trusts him with everything, including herself. He's so gentle, she knows he'll make it worth it.

Later that night…….

Thomas walks into Savannah's apartment with a duffle bag full of fresh clothes. After closing the door, he stops to take in the sight. Lit candles are everywhere. "How did you do all this in thirty minutes?" He yells towards the bathroom that she seems to be occupying. When did she get candles? Where was she able to hide all of these without him seeing?

Once the bathroom door opens, his mouth drops. Savannah is standing there in a red lacey push-up bra and mouth-watering underwear. Her blonde hair shimmering from the reflection of the candles. Her nervous eyes watching intensely for a reaction. "Savannah," he pleads hoarsely. His mouth suddenly feels very dry.

Instead of saying anything, she walks toward him. Taking his duffle bag, she drops it on the floor and pulls him in for a kiss. Softly at first, then deeply once he begins to match her. Pulling away, she begins kissing him along his neck to mimic what he's been doing to her these past few weeks. Taking his groans as encouragement, she continues to kiss. Adding a trail with her tongue along his adam's apple. When she reaches the other side of his neck, she bites down. He grabs her by the ass and pulls her roughly against his hardening cock. "Did that hurt?" She asks with hesitation.

"Not even close," he groans.

Her hands begin to explore his body. Realizing it's a little tough to do with his clothes on, she begins at the hem and pushes his shirt up, grazing her fingers along his skin, and lifting the shirt over his head. As she begins to unbuckle his belt, his hands still hers.

"Savannah," he groans, "I don't think I can stop myself if you take it out."

Instead of replying, Savannah unbuttons his pants and pulls them down as she gets on her knees. Grabbing his cock, she starts placing soft kisses along the shaft to the tip. Gaining courage, she starts by putting his head in her mouth. She's done this before but now it's different. As much as she wants this to happen, she still can't stop trembling with nervousness. Taking more and more of him in her mouth with each bob of her head. Even with this angle, she won't be able to take all of him. It isn't for lack of trying. She's never been able to stuff her mouth.

He gasps. "Oh, shit!"

She feels him grab her hair, then let go. He's still afraid to touch her. Grabbing one of his hands, she places it on the side of her head to encourage him to touch her. Slowly, he begins to sink his fingers in her hair and grab hold.

"Savannah?" She hears him call out in a husky voice. "Hmmm," her voice vibrates along his cock.

He pulls himself out of her mouth and pulls her to her feet. He places a deep kiss on her lips while his hands softly trail her body, then gripping with need. Even though he's gentle, she can feel his desire for her radiating through his body. "If you continue to touch me, I won't be able to stop myself from making you mine," he warns.

She takes a long look at him and notices that he is shaved. He's so devilishly handsome. His respect for her stirs her insides even more. Grabbing his hand, she leads the way to the bed. "Good," she says seductively as she nears it.

"Savannah?" He stops and questions her decision with only one word.

"I'm ready to be yours," she whispers while looking into his eyes. Before he can respond, she turns to walk the last few feet to the bed.

He is behind her with such a swiftness it startles her. He reaches around with one hand to slip into her underwear and start massaging her clit, while the other hand begins cupping her breast with a firm squeeze. Trailing soft kisses along the back of her neck, "you're so beautiful," he hoarsely whispers. Bringing a hand back around, he unhooks her bra. Spinning her around to face him, he slides the bra off with such quickness. Sucking air through his teeth at the sight of her breast bouncing out of their confinement. Bending forward, he puts the right breast in his mouth while one of his hands returns to rub her clit. She needs to be wet and ready for him. He doesn't want to give her more pain than she will already be in when he breaks through. The smell of her readiness makes his cock jump.

She moans loudly at his touch. "I don't know how much better it can feel compared to this."

He chuckles with her nipple in his mouth. Nibbling harder than his recent ministrations. He felt the moment her knees began to buckle. She grabs ahold of his head to steady herself. He can tell she wasn't expecting that. As he begins to work on her other breast, he can feel her body begin to tighten as her hands hold onto his head more firmly. Switching positions, he moves to his knees to taste her while his hand goes to fondle her breast.

"Thomas, I won't be able to hold myself up for much longer," she says while gasping.

He continues to do as he's been. He moves an arm around her waist to support her when she's ready to crumble. It didn't take long for her to crumble once he put his mouth between her legs. If he wasn't holding her up, she would've collapsed onto the floor. When she shattered, both of her knees buckled. She even grabbed his shoulders in an attempt to hold herself up. Once she reached her peak, he stops what he was doing. Still holding onto her, he stands up to give her a kiss that signifies they aren't done yet. He needs her like he needs air for his lungs. No clue how long he'll last, but he is hoping she'll understand. He wanted to make a lasting impression for her first time. Wanted to take his time with her. His need for her has ruined his patience.

Placing Savannah on the bed, he begins to pull her underwear completely off. As he leans in, he places soft kisses on her hips. Standing up, he peruses the length of her body. His eyes stop at the delicious spot between her legs and decide to taste her some more. Taking his tongue, he begins to lick between her lips once more. Once they're sufficiently parted, he begins to suck on her clit.

She grabs him by the hair and pulls him up to face her. "Stop! Now you're just prolonging the tortuous wait. I want you now!"

He stands up. With a smile, he says, "yes ma'am!" He can feel her eyes on him as he makes his way to his side of the bed. In the nightstand he's occupied since she returned from the hospital after the kidnapping, he pulls out a condom.

"When did you put those there?" She asks with eyes filled with amazement.

"I can't divulge all my secrets," replying with a wink.

She watches him with curiosity as he rolls the condom onto his cock. "Does it hurt?"

"It's uncomfortable, but not painful," he answers without a tease. Crawling into bed and hovering over her, he orders, "spread em." Savannah snorts with amusement and puts a smile on her face while doing as she's told. Giving her a deep kiss on her lips while he puts himself into position at her entrance. Her very warm and wet entrance. With hesitation, he says, "let me know if this hurts too much."

"Don't worry, I won't," she teases. As he begins to pull away, she wraps her legs around his waist to hold him in place. Grabbing his cock, she begins to stroke it. "I wouldn't know the answer to this, but wouldn't it feel better inside of me, than using my hand?"

Instead of answering, he takes himself and begins to tease her entrance. "You're so fucking wet," he struggles to speak and places his head on her collarbone. Slowly getting the head inside of her small entrance, "you're so tight. I might explode just from this."

Gasping at the feeling of penetration, she demands, "more!"

Thomas pushes in and out. Slowly going deeper until he feels resistance. Taking her mouth with his, he begins to kiss her deeply. Pushing past the resistance as he moans into her mouth. The feel of her is exquisite. When she lets out a gasp, he asks, "did that hurt?"

"Nope, just surprised me. Are we done?" Savannah asks with confusion. If this is what every guy raves about, no wonder the girls aren't...... Oh!

Are we done? I'll show her! Thomas begins to move in and out of her as she looks to him to answer her question. With every movement, it becomes harder and harder to hold himself together. With any other girl, he would be able to last.

With her, he knew deep down that he wouldn't last very long during their first time together. The anticipation has been building up ever since he decided he was going to make her his. "You're. Mine," he punctuates with each thrust.

"Faster!" Savannah demands while squirming beneath him.

Trying very hard to concentrate on lasting, he found it in himself to pump faster. "Say it, Savannah," he grunts. Pumping faster and faster until he feels her tighten her whole body, then hears it, "yours!" She moans with pleasure. When he feels her contract around him, it becomes his undoing. Loudly moaning his pleasure, while not giving a damn about their coworkers who live next door. He leans in for a deep kiss to end their actions before he falls into the spot next to her. Even though she might be healed enough for this, she's not ready for the weight of him. She's so petite compared to him. He'll feel as if he's suffocating her.

"That was incredible! Can we do it again?" She asks enthusiastically. Seriously the best thing she has ever felt. It didn't hurt at all or feel the way her friends described it. Is it different for everyone? How is that possible if all her friends shared similar experiences in high school? She thought she couldn't feel more pleasure than when he was at her breast. Man, was she wrong. Can it get better than it just did?

He laughs. "You gotta give me a bit. If you still want to, then absolutely!" The feel of her was unlike anything he's ever experienced. Being inside her feels as if she was made for him.

She never cried out in pain as he went deep. Not as deep as he could've, but deep. It will be a fun experiment to see how much of him can fit inside of her. Once she's accustomed to him, of course. She'll already be sore after her first time. She might not feel it yet, but come morning she will. Her enthusiasm excites him. The things he'll be able to do and teach her.

Chapter Twenty-Four

Last night had to be the best night of her life. Three times. Between Thomas needing a break and his insistence that she ices her vagina to prevent it from being too sore, they had sex three times before finally falling asleep. She can recall every detail of their night. Every touch, every word, and every look they shared. He helped make the night a wonderful memory by caring about her.

"I can hardly sit without wincing," Savannah shares. For what purpose? She has no idea since the words just fell out of her mouth.

He chuckles. "You're the one who wouldn't go to bed. I'm not complaining in the least bit. I slept like a rock."

"I know. You snored the whole night. It was louder than us during sex," she laughs. "Is that ice trick something you used on the last virgin you had sex with?" She asks with curiosity and hoping she's hiding her hint of jealousy.

He whips his head towards her to assess her meaning. After a moment, he goes back to mucking the stalls. "You're the only virgin I've been with. The ice trick works for any female who has lots of sex."

"Oh," responding with a tone of disappointment.

He leans the pitchfork against the stall and walks toward her. "What?"

"Nothing," she answers while shaking her head.

"Savannah," he says in a stern voice.

"Ew. That sounded like my dad," she says with a face full of disgust.

"Please tell me why your mood just changed?" He asks while guiding her chin to make her look at him.

"I just don't like to imagine you having lots of sex with numerous women," she says with embarrassment on her face.

He laughs. "Numerous women might be an overstatement. I've had practice, yes. Practice with people I've been in relationships with. I'm very picky about whom I bed."

"Where do I fit in your picky decision-making?" She asks quietly.

"You're much too beautiful to be lacking confidence," he informs as he pulls her close and begins to kiss her. "I'm the lucky one. I don't know what I did right to be given this opportunity."

"That doesn't answer my question." Fighting very hard against his distractions to receive the answer she's been fishing for. She needs to feel special. She's never felt special with a guy she's dated.

"You are mine, Savannah. Mine. I'm all yours. I don't share, understand?" He says firmly.

She nods her head, then places a kiss on his cheek. Just as she pulls away, she sees her aunt walk in.

"Hey now, let's keep it professional!" Kate says with an arch in her brow.

"Oh, yeah? Daddy told me about a particular scene he walked in on with you and uncle Noah," Savannah snorts. When he shared that particular tidbit, she thought it was scandalous. She didn't think her aunt had it in her.

"First of all, I'm going to strangle him for telling you. Second of all, do as I say and not as I do. Let's go for a walk, Savannah," Kate urges. She watches as Savannah walks out the door. As they clear the barn, she whispers, "I see your plan worked."

"How did you know?" She asks with widening eyes.

"Your walk gives you away," Kate whispers.

"My walk?" Savannah questions as she begins to overthink her movements.

"It's a kind of walk females have when they're sore between the legs," Kate shrugs.

"Oh, no! Are you disappointed in me?" Savannah asks with her head tilted towards the floor. Kate is the one person she doesn't want to disappoint. Even though she had asked for her advice, she didn't think about anything past her goal. Also didn't expect to be discussing her success.

"Never. I'm impressed you've held out this long. You're a grown woman who can make her own decisions. I surely didn't wait until your age. I was a bit reckless," Kate answers with a laugh.

"Why are we walking?" Savannah questions. Not seeming to be heading anywhere in particular.

"I'm giving you the chance to talk about anything you'd like. We can also walk in silence the whole time if you would prefer that. Regardless, I'm craving your company," Kate answers with a smile.

After walking for a bit in silence, Savannah asks the question that's been weighing on her mind, "what did it feel like to shoot him?" When she returned home from the kidnapping, her dreams included doing just that.

"I didn't relish in doing so. It all happened so quickly. I asked him to stop. Who knows what he would've done if he knocked the gun out of my hands? I didn't want to wait around and find out," Kate answers.

"Do you regret it?" Savannah wonders aloud. Would she have regretted it if she was in her shoes? After what they did to her, she doesn't think she would have.

"I regret not beating them further with the baton. It's funny, kind of, I don't feel remorse about ending his life. I'm sure a psychologist would have a lot to say about that. I did what I felt I needed to do to protect myself and my family," Kate answers with complete honesty. If one person is deserving of it, it is Savannah.

"Why have I had such bad luck in life?" Savannah questions with sadness in her voice.

"Oh, honey. This world is so cruel. Even more so for females. I, too, have had my share of bad experiences. This life I've built here is my escape from the reminders of it. I still remember them, and I expect I always will, but I don't need the continuous reminders the city was providing me," Kate says in an attempt to comfort.

"You're lucky to have Noah," Savannah returns.

"We're lucky to have each other. In a way, we saved each other when we needed it the most. I've sadly kissed a lot of frogs before I found my king," Kate corrects with a smile.

"That's not how the saying goes," Savannah laughs.

"No? Well, my version is so much better," Kate teases. "You and Thomas are lucky to have each other as well. Life won't always be this difficult," she encourages.

"Thomas is the only reason I sleep at night. I'm terrified to be alone. I'm also terrified that I need him so much," Savannah admits softly.

"That's a normal feeling. I couldn't imagine you not being terrified. I'm glad he's been here for you. I've always liked Thomas. But you should always know that we're also here for you. My door is always open if you want to sleep in the house with us," Kate offers with sweetness in her voice.

Savannah smiles at her. Kate has always been there to step up when her mom was lacking. Kate is still doing it even now that she's reached adulthood. "I don't know if I want to go back to dads house."

"You're a grown-up now. You're allowed to make your own choices. Once you've healed up a bit more, I'd be more than happy to employ you," Kate returns with an even bigger smile while throwing her arm over Savannah's shoulder.

"Daddy won't like my decision," Savannah says while leaning against her.

"Let me worry about my brother," Kate says while giving Savannah's arm a gentle squeeze.

Chapter Twenty-Five

Ever since the party at Thomas' house that she showed up uninvited to, Savannah hasn't been able to get the image of her sitting on his lap out of her head. Wondering how it would feel to have sex in that position? They've had sex in the bed a lot and even once in the shower. Never in a chair. Granted, it's only been a few days since she gave herself to him, but she hasn't been able to think about anything other than sex. About all the ways they can be intimate. She's flexible and Thomas is strong. Surely that's a good combination for numerous positions? How many positions are there? She doesn't want to ask anyone. She's too embarrassed to even get caught searching for the answer on the internet.

As she finishes up in the shower, she decides to just go for it. Turning the shower off, she steps out and begins to pat herself dry. Once that's complete, she decides to emerge from the bathroom without a towel. She's never done it before and wonders how he'll react. As she emerges from the bathroom, she scans the room and spots him in a chair tying his shoes. Walking toward him, he finally notices once she's halfway to him.

Sitting up and ignoring his other laces, he sucks air in through his teeth, "damn, look at that perfection."

Instead of rolling her eyes which would get her a scolding, she says nothing as she continues toward him. She watches as his eyes watch her with interest. A beautiful smile across his face. He is so handsome that she can't even believe he's real at times. Without asking, she straddles his lap. It's a shame he's fully dressed. Leaning in, she kisses him. Soft and gentle at first, then desperate with need.

"Does this mean you've changed your mind about the movie?" He asks once she begins trailing kisses along his neck. Without answering, she begins to pull his shirt over his head. "Let's go to the bed," he suggests as he pulls her in tighter. Running a hand down her back while the other travels up her neck and grabs her hair to pull her in for a rougher kiss and groans loudly.

"Nope," she lets out as she scoots back to unbutton his jeans. Hoping off his lap she orders, "stand." When he does as he's told, she gets onto her knees while pulling his pants and boxers down along the way. His already hard cock springs free to greet her in the face. She eagerly grabs it and wraps her lips around it and begins sucking.

He had to stop his knees from buckling at the intense feeling of her eagerness. He sits back down on the chair and grabs the back of her head to bring her mouth back onto his cock. Groaning loudly once more as she begins to suck harder. He grabs each side of her face to bring her lower onto him and make her swallow more of him. "Open wider," he orders. She opens up as wide as she can go to allow him to shove as much as he can in her mouth. He gets another few inches in until she begins to gag. Pulling her mouth off of him to give her a chance to get some air, he then places one hand around her throat. Squeezing slightly to apply pressure, he leads her up off of her knees and pulls her forward to straddle him. What started as her taking control turned into him finally finding out how she reacts to being choked. So far, she hasn't shown any objections.

Pulling her by the throat to look into her eyes, he says in a hoarse voice, "your mouth may not be able to fit all of me, but your pussy will." She places his cock away from her entrance to make his shaft rub against her clit to stimulate her while she grinds on him. "Where's the condom?" He groans as he struggles to form words. Releasing her neck as he begins to look around the room for the box he just brought over.

"Wait, this feels incredible," she says while beginning to grind faster.

"You're so wet. I want you to fuck me now," he demands.

One little hop up and his cock springs to the perfect position for her to land on top of his head. Didn't take much for her to begin sliding down and swallow him with her slippery entrance. Savannah can't help but think how much better he feels inside of her without a condom. Before he puts a stop to it, she decides to take full advantage of this feeling.

Once he's fully inside of her, she begins to grind back and forth.

"Savannah," he groans, "you're so fucking wet and warm."

Smiling, "this feels so much better," she says as she begins to grind faster. "I can feel your smooth skin inside of me."

"Savannah," he hoarsely whispers while grabbing each ass cheek with his hands to move her even faster.

She positions her feet on the chair so she can spread her legs wider and take every inch of him. Gasping at the depth he reaches, "I feel as if you're in my stomach."

He groans loudly with pleasure at her description. "You're so fucking perfect. Tight, soaking wet, and you've managed to swallow me whole."

"Thomas, you're so big. I can't hold on," she cries out.

"What every guy wants to hear," he chuckles as he grabs her by the throat again. Pressing just enough to increase her pleasure and ensure she reaches her peak before he does. He won't be able to hold back much longer.

Within minutes, she cries out in pleasure while exploding all over his bare cock. "My turn," he says as he picks her up. Walking over to the bed, he lays her back on the mattress with her ass about to hang off of it. He grabs a pillow and places it underneath her ass and orders, "hold your ankles."

As soon as she did what she was told, he shoves himself back into her without warning and she gasps at the abruptness. As he slams in and out of her, he presses that particular spot on her lower stomach to increase pleasure. After what seemed like an eternity, his patience is rewarded when she squirts all over him. The look of horror in her eyes made him grin and pump furiously.

"Thomas?" She questions with a soft voice of embarrassment.

Leaning closer to her while he's pumping away, he grabs her head to pull her in for a deep kiss. Letting go, he quickly pulls himself out of her and explodes all over her stomach. Moaning loudly as he strokes the last out of himself. "Fuck! That was amazing!"

"You enjoy being peed on?" She asks as she looks at him with widening eyes.

He begins laughing. "No, that's not what just happened. Squirting is a different way to orgasm."

"Oh," she says as she pauses to think. "The choking made things feel more intense."

"I was counting on it to do just that," he grins. "Did you enjoy it?"

"I did," she says with hesitation. After a brief pause, "I also like the sweet and loving sex. Is that okay?" She asks softly.

Thomas walks back over to her after retrieving a towel to clean her up. He leans towards her and places a gentle kiss on her lips, "I like that kind also. If I try stuff and you don't like it, tell me to stop. You don't have to go along with anything just to please me. That'll make me feel like shit. Okay?"

Savannah nods. "I did like it. Just not for every time." Why is it that she enjoys Thomas being rough? Why is it that she also feels a bit uncomfortable knowing when he handles her as such, it brings pleasure? Is it too soon to delve into this type of sex after she was kidnapped?

Smiling once more. After he finishes wiping her up, he tosses the towel across the room. He picks her up off of the bed and heads to the bathroom. "Let's go take a shower. I need to lather you up."

Chapter Twenty-Six

Walking into Savannah's apartment he catches sight of her examining her outfit in the body-length mirror. She looks amazing. The contrast of her tan along with the skin-tight white dress makes the white even brighter. Her long blonde hair he enjoys pulling is flowing down her back. Her dress is a little shorter than he would like for hanging out with his friends, but it'll be fine. He'll be there to hold her the whole night and claim her as his. The makeup makes her lavender eyes stand out even more. He would prefer her to not wear makeup, but she always insists. Instead of announcing his entrance, he leans against the wall to watch her get ready. Perfection at its finest.

"You just admiring the view?" Savannah asks over her shoulder with a wink.

"Absolutely. Do you need to change? I can help you dispose of your clothes. You look (sucking air through his teeth) stunning in that dress, but I'll always prefer you au natural," he says seductively as he walks toward her.

"Don't you dare! It took me too long to choose this outfit to begin with," she warns as she tries to evade his reach. She has a surprise and doesn't want him to spoil it.

Thomas grabs her around the waist and pulls her to him. "You smell so good," he says while taking a deep inhale of her neck. Slowly, he begins placing kisses along her neckline.

"That's what happens when one takes a shower," she teases.

"Do we have to go to this dinner? I already know what I'd like to eat," he teases back as he spins her to view her ass. Taking his hand, he lands a dominating slap on it. "So perfect," he admires while ending with a squeeze.

"They're your friends, so yes. Let's go or we'll be late," she lightly scolds while tugging him behind her. Grabbing her purse, she pulls him through the doorway. She's never worn this dress before. It has been amongst her clothes for almost a year and she's only now feeling comfortable enough to wear it. The reaction Thomas just gave, pleased her immensely about her choice.

"No bending over at the party. I'll pick up whatever you drop. I can almost see your ass as is," he says while bending over to try and see underneath her dress.

She quickly turns to prevent him from looking under her dress. "Access denied," she teases.

He reaches out as if he's going to open the door for her and instead spins her around to face him. Pulling her tightly to him, he kisses her with a hungry desire. "Please, can we just stay home?" He asks with a rasp.

"I like the begging," she says with a finger to her chin to ponder what he asked. "No," she says as she reaches to open her door. She can feel his desire poking her through their clothes.

He holds the door firmly closed, "you're not allowed to open your own door. That's my job." As she steps away, he opens the door to allow her in. After she gets in carefully, she looks up at him and smiles in a way that says she holding something back. The walk around the car gave him a minute to ponder what it could be. Deciding it was nothing more than flirtation, he gets into the driver's seat.

After a quick ten-minute drive, they show up at a country house. Well, a house she would still call country, but in this town, it would be what someone would call a house in the suburbs. Not enough property to be farmland, but more of a yard than a suburban house in the big city would have. Cute houses along the block that have similar features. What a cute attempt, she thought.

As they pull into the driveway, he looks toward Savannah. "There might be one of my high school exes at the dinner. A guy who I used to be friends with is supposedly dating her. I didn't break it off in the nicest way."

"I'll be fine, thanks for the heads up," she says sincerely while grabbing his hand and placing it on her lap. "I've been keeping this a secret," whispering playfully as she guides his hand between her legs.

Once he feels it, his eyes widen. "You're not wearing any underwear," he hisses, "we're going home. Now!"

She quickly jumps out of the car and runs up the stairs while laughing. Ringing the doorbell as she watches Thomas get out of the car as coolly as he can with irritation on his face as he walks toward her. With a huge grin on her face, she rings the doorbell once more. Hopefully, they'll answer before he has a chance to give his two cents.

"Get in the car, Savannah," he commands.

"No, this is more fun. This might be the only way I can tease you and have power," she replies with a wink.

"You want power? If we go home, I'll let you tie me to the bed," he bribes.

She pauses, "tie you?" She questions out loud to herself. Opening her mouth once more just to close it. After a few moments, she asks, "what's that like?" Just then the door opens up to a woman and a man who appear to be their age. The man appears to be lacking in the looks department when she compares him to Thomas. It's not fair of her to judge. She is biased in her opinion that Thomas is hotter than any man she has ever seen. The woman standing next to him is beautiful. She has long brown hair, deep blue eyes, makeup is done to perfection, is tall, slim and her designer clothes suggest she doesn't live in the country with the rest of them. She must be visiting someone here. Feeling the tension in the air, Savannah giggles at the knowledge that Thomas is full of irritation.

"Rachel, you're looking well," Thomas greets.

"Fuck off!" Rachel retorts before walking off.

Thomas eyes Savannah as she snorts in amusement. "Good ole Rachel. What's up, Matt? This is my girlfriend, Savannah."

Savannah turns her head quickly towards Thomas and eyes him with a questioning look. After they exchange their greetings, Thomas ushers Savannah into the house with one hand on her lower back. There's no way he's letting her out of his reach now that he knows she is going commando.

"Girlfriend?" Savannah whispers.

Thomas leans in, "You're mine, I've already said as much. I wouldn't have fucked you if I wasn't planning on being with you." He pauses to smile at another friend before he leans back into her ear, "if you think the door saved you from me, you're wrong. I'm tempted to pull you into the bathroom and rip your dress off. Seeing as how we're at a friend's house, I'll think of a different punishment."

She's blushing deeply now. She wasn't aware they were official. Yes, they have been playing the part. It just all became very real when he introduced her. "Can I honestly tie you to the bed?" She asks in a whisper.

"I might tie you instead to punish you. Faced in a way that I can still spank you for this little stunt. It's a good thing I'm wearing loose pants since I'm so fucking hard right now. It wouldn't take much to slide myself underneath that dress and fuck the shit out of you," he whispers hoarsely, "did you shave every bit?"

"Then my power of seduction is strong tonight," she teases. Ignoring his question increased his irritation. Punishment? What would that entail?

"Savannah," he warns.

With another giggle, she walks toward the group of people with him hot on her heels. "Hello, Leo. Where's Gabe?"

"He didn't want to come tonight," Leo leans in and whispers, "Gabe and Rachel don't get along."

The level of jealousy Thomas is feeling towards his friend is unnecessary. Watching him lean in and whisper a secret into Savannah's ear made him want to shove him away. Maybe it's knowing Savannah is commando? Maybe it's because he knows Leo wanted to ask her out at his party. This woman is changing him. In the past, he wouldn't have batted an eye. He trusts her. He just doesn't trust the other people near her.

As they sit down to eat, Savannah makes sure to take a seat between Leo and Thomas. She can tell he's weirdly jealous. She just wanted to avoid sitting next to someone she didn't know. Most importantly, not next to Rachel. Every time Thomas reaches over to put his hand near her entrance, she grabs his hand to hold instead. Denying him the chance to touch or tease her. This night is about teasing him. About holding the power she's yet been able to hold while with him. She loves when he takes control. Her curiosity about taking control has now given her a different form of desire. The desire to make him want her so bad he aches for her. Aching so bad it takes all of his efforts to not give in to the desire with a group of people in the next room. What would it be like to sneak off and have her way with him at a party? To be forced to remain silent so no one is aware of the pleasure she is receiving. Would that even be possible? Could they get away unnoticed in a gathering this small?

Dinner went smoothly. She noticed Rachel kept eyeing her throughout the meal. Does she still wish to be with Thomas? She hardly saw Rachel in conversation with her current boyfriend. The mental image of the two of them together irritates her. Thomas belongs to her and has said as much.

As they were saying their goodbyes, Rachel pulls Savannah to the side. "Don't let Thomas fool you, he's a major asshole. He doesn't give a shit about you unless you're in bed together," she scoffs. "Once he's had his fill, he'll move on to someone else."

"People change. Not everyone you date is the right person for you. Thank you for being the wrong person for him," Savannah retorts before she turns to walk away. She had to walk away. She's never wanted to be the girl who fights someone over jealousy. Never thought it was an attractive quality.

Thomas watches the whole exchange from a distance. Watching Savannah walk away and leave Rachel with a gaping mouth, makes him smile. His smile becomes even larger when Savannah changes direction to make a beeline for him. As she reaches him, she pulls his shirt towards her for a deep kiss. "I'm ready," he hears her whisper. Was the kiss because of desire or to show Rachel up?

As they get into the car and start to drive off, he asks, "what was that about?"

"She said you're an asshole who only gives a shit while you're in bed with me," she says with a shrug. "That you'll leave me once you've had your fill."

"What did you say?" He asks with a side-eye.

"I thanked her for being the wrong person for you," she says with a smile. She watches him laugh. Hard. He's so damn handsome and she can't handle it. He has such a perfect smile and the sound is music to her ears. It oddly pleases her that he's so amused by her words. She smiles brightly when he reaches over to hold her hand as they drive the short distance to the farm.

"Did she divulge that I broke up with her because I had my fill of the number of times she cheated on me?" He asks. Needing her to understand what happened in high school.

"Of course not. That would show she was at fault," she begins smiling brightly. Even though she trusts him unreservedly, it makes her feel better about herself to hear how terrible of a person this Rachel girl truly is.

As they walk into her apartment, he closes the door behind them and locks it. Grabbing her by the waist, he pulls her back to pin her against the wall. Kissing her deeply while pressing all of himself against her.

She moans against his mouth. She can feel his rock-hard cock pressing into her. The power of his whole body is such a turn-on for her. Suddenly, she's lifted in the air while still against the wall and feels his body press deeper into her. He has her legs wrapped around his waist while he's supporting her ass with one of his forearms.

Using his other arm, he undoes his belt and zipper. While continuing to kiss her, he lets his pants fall to his knees as he pulls himself free from his boxers. Letting it hang, he takes four fingers and puts them into her mouth as he pulls his mouth away. "Wet them. Lick and suck them like you would my cock," he orders. Not quite sure if she nodded or if it was simply a bob of her head, but she is obeying. Feeling sufficiently wet, he replaces his fingers with his mouth. Kissing her deeply once more. He reaches down to put her saliva on the tip of his cock and groans from the feel of it. Readying himself at her entrance, he then shoves himself inside of her as he lowers her.

"Fuck!" He exclaims at the incredible sensation. He hears her gasp at the abruptness. It's a good gasp since it is quickly replaced with moans of pleasure. He can get much deeper at this angle. Since they're not in a soft bed, there's no give with the wall. He can push deeper and not have her sink away from him. "Hold on," he urges as he hooks one arm under each of her legs to open her up to him even more.

So deep. He's so fucking deep and she can't even catch her breath. This desire he has to be inside of her makes it all the more thrilling when he's forceful. He does things she never even thought possible. Things she wouldn't imagine enjoying if her friends had shared such stories. It's as if he knows what she wants before she even knows she wants them. "Thomas, I can't hold on, I'm going to slip," she cries out. Is slipping even possible when he's pressing her so forcefully against the wall?

As she feels him begin to pump harder and faster, she begins to feel the buildup. Her arms are wrapped around his neck as she holds on as best as she can. Her whole body tightens with the slightest tinge of annoyance until she explodes. Explodes all around him as she constricts around his cock while losing her grip on his neck.

After she cries out in pleasure, he quickly lowers her to the ground. "Quickly get on your knees and open your mouth," he orders. She does as she's told with barely enough time for him to put his cock in her mouth before exploding inside of it. Without being told to, she starts sucking to get all of it out. "Fuck! You're so perfect," he moans. As he helps her up, he looks into her eyes, "seriously, you're perfect, Savannah." After noticing she swallowed what was in her mouth, he turns her around and roughly spanks her once, "a fitting punishment."

"This was my punishment? I think I'll misbehave even more now. That was so much fun!" She teases with amusement as she walks away.

He watches with an open mouth as she begins to peel her dress off while walking away. With nothing left to cover her, she walks over to the sink and begins to brush her teeth. "I've created a monster," he chuckles.

Chapter Twenty-Seven

knock, knock, knock

"Just a minute!" Savannah yells.

"Who could that be?" Thomas asks.

"I have no idea," she returns while throwing a pair of pajama pants at him. "Put that away," she returns while gesturing with her hands toward his cock.

knock, knock, knock

Savannah throws the door open as she says with irritation, "impatient much?"

"Excuse me?" Dylan snaps with anger.

"Daddy!" Savannah squeaks. "I didn't know it was you before I said it."

"Is this how you greet people in the country?" Dylan asks with suspicion on his face.

"No," Savannah replies while grabbing her phone as she steps outside and begins to close the door, "let's go eat breakfast at aunt Kate's."

Pushing the door fully open, Dylan interrupts, "I want to see your apartment." Stepping inside her apartment, he spots a familiar young man whose half naked.

With nothing left to do but get ready for what's assuredly going to come next, Savannah pulls out her phone to text Kate. *Daddy's in my apt, help!* Savannah knew the second her dad spotted Thomas.

"I didn't send you to the country to become a harlot," Dylan roars.

Thomas advances toward Dylan, but Savannah stops him by blocking with her body.

"Is opening your legs to him how you thanked him for saving you at the party?" Dylan insults.

"Daddy, please stop. That's not what this is," Savannah pleads. "He's my boyfriend, now."

Kate rushes to the door just as Dylan prepares his next blow, "boyfriend? Since when do you open your legs to your boyfriends? Whatever happened to you saving yourself for marriage like your mother and I taught you? Did he even save you at the fraternity party? Were you honestly there looking for just this?" Dylan accuses with a flail of his hands towards Thomas' bare chest.

"Don't you dare speak to her like that," Thomas seethes.

"I raised this little harlot. I can say whatever the fuck I want to her," Dylan roars.

"Whoa! As much as I don't want to intrude on a parent disciplining their child, I will not tolerate abuse in any form," Kate raises her voice as she walks to stand in front of her brother.

"Taught her all your ways, Kate?" Dylan accuses.

"In how to be a decent person? Absolutely!" Kate bites back.

"On how to spread her legs to every guy who will treat her badly. You've got enough experience in that," verbally attacking her where it'll hurt the most. Kate slaps him across the face. "I shouldn't have saved you that night, you bitch!" Dylan roars as he raises his arm to hit her.

Dylan is about to slap her when his hand is grabbed. Turning around to punch whoever is restraining his wrist, but instead makes contact with a fist to his face. Unfortunately, the one punch to his face didn't take him down. Disorients him for a bit, but he quickly opens his eyes to swing again. Noah shoves the fist away with his forearm and gives Dylan an uppercut. The uppercut finally knocks him down. Noah looks over to find Kate comforting a crying Savannah in the corner of the room while Thomas is standing to the side watching the exchange. "Stay down, Dylan," Noah warns.

He didn't stay down for very long. Dylan gets up and charges toward Noah. Noah ducks under and throws his shoulder into Dylan's stomach. Quickly standing up and adding a knee to his stomach as he's bent over holding himself from the first blow. Dylan groans in pain as he falls to the floor. "Stay down," Noah warns again with anger.

"Fuck you," Dylan tries with conviction while wheezing.

"Nah," Noah shrugs, "now, I don't know what happened, but I wasn't about to let you hit my wife."

"Dylan just bought himself a one-way ticket out of my life with his choice of words," Kate yells across the room.

"Fine by me! I'm taking my daughter with me when I go. Savannah, pack your bags," Dylan says as he tries to pick himself up off of the floor.

"No!" Savannah yells.

"Excuse me? Pack. Your. Bags!" Dylan attempts to roar. His voice is not quite back.

"No. I'm staying here," Savannah says with conviction through her tears.

"With your whore of an aunt?" Dylan asks loudly.

Before Noah can react, Thomas punches Dylan on the side of his face and lays him flat. "That felt good," he groans while rubbing his knuckles.

As Dylan lays on the floor groaning, Kate says, "looks like this whore keeps pretty good company. Now, get off my property and out of my life."

Dylan didn't even attempt to fight when Noah took it upon himself to grab him with one arm held behind his back to shove him out of the apartment towards the driveway.

"You own the ranch?" Thomas asks.

"Technically, Noah now owns half, but yes," Kate answers.

"That's pretty badass!" Thomas exclaims.

Savannah runs towards Thomas and jumps into his arms and wraps her legs around his waist. "Thank you, for everything."

Holding her body up with one forearm underneath her ass, he uses the other to sink into her hair to pull her forward and kiss her forehead. "I didn't know we could punch him. I would've done it before Noah got here. You missed some pretty harsh insults he spat at Savannah," Thomas says with irritation while holding her tightly.

Kate laughs. "When you're defending Savannah's honor, swing away." Heading out the door, she stops to look back, "thank you, Thomas. The love you have for my niece is much appreciated." Without waiting for a response, she walks out and heads toward the house. She needs to make sure Noah has it in hand.

Walking up to Noah with purpose, Kate throws herself into him and nearly knocks him over in the process and kisses him fervently. Coming up for air she says, "thank you."

"You want to thank me? I have other wicked ideas in mind instead of words," Noah says with a wink and a devilishly handsome grin.

The things that face does to her insides. "I already do the wicked things. Does this mean I have some banked?" Kate says with excitement. His eyes. The things his beautiful silver eyes do to her. His looks always make her ache with need.

"Nope. Your credit expires after an hour," he teases as he begins to nip at her throat. He feels Kate sink her hands into his hair to encourage him further.

"Those are some harsh rules, Mr. Banker, Sir," she says playfully as her insides begin to catch fire from his attention.

Noah pulls his head back and looks into her eyes, "we can discuss payment inside my office. It's my break time and I'm starving," he suggests with a hungry stare.

"You might have to catch me first," she squeals with excitement as she runs inside the house.

"One….. Two….. Three….. Four!" Noah counts out loud before he gives chase.

Chapter Twenty-Eight

After Kate said what she did, neither of them said anything for a few minutes. What is he supposed to say? Is he supposed to profess his feelings? Is this love? Damn Kate for making the situation more awkward than it needed to be. Is Savannah ready to say those three words? How does one bring up a conversation like that? Thomas thought he was in love before and it was all wrong. He doesn't want to be wrong about Savannah or give her the wrong idea if that's not what this is.

Instead of saying anything about it at all, he decides to take another route by ignoring it completely. Maybe she never heard what her aunt said. Maybe she'll forget if he changes the subject? "Is that normal behavior for your dad?" He asks with irritation. He can't get over what just happened.

"He's never been that angry," she says while still sniffling. To insult her in front of people is a new low.

"What about the insults?" He asks while trying to keep his irritation and anger in check. Looking toward her, he notices tears glistening on her cheeks and the sadness in her eyes. How can a parent treat their child as such?

"Towards me? Yes. I've never been good enough for him. My younger sister is his golden child," she admits somberly. Never good enough. Hence the reason for her own desire to be perfect.

"Now I understand why you felt so insecure and thought I was rejecting you. I don't understand how anyone could reject you. You have no idea how incredible you are," he says while pulling her in to hold.

"My sister even had a pregnancy scare. I got blamed for not watching her closely enough. She's two years younger than I am. She got coddled while I got grounded," she admits with an eye roll. Purposely ignoring the compliment that she doesn't agree with. He's the incredible one. She wouldn't have made it through the past few weeks without him.

"That's such bullshit," he says with anger seeping through. "What can I do to cheer you up?"

"Can we go to your house? I need a change of scenery." Internally fearful that her dad will somehow make it back inside.

"Sure. Let me collect my dirty clothes. I could use some clean clothes anyways," he says while looking around the room.

Ten minutes later……..

As they walk into his room she asks, "are your parents home?"

"No, they're at work," he answers while dropping his dirty clothes into his hamper.

"I know how you can cheer me up," she says while sauntering over to him.

Eyeing her suspiciously, "name it."

"Well," she places a kiss on his lips, then begins to trail them down his neck, "I was thinking."

"Yes?" He drawls with suspicion.

"That I would like to know what it's like to tie you up," she says with a smile against his neck.

"Usually I do the tying," he says with a husky voice while pulling her hair to make her head fall back and expose her neck. With a hand on her lower back, he begins to press her against him. Leaning in, he places a kiss on the exposed skin. After a few soft kisses, he begins to trail his tongue along the side of her neck.

"I'm not like the other girls. I want to tie YOU up," she insists while pulling his hair.

Pulling back to look at her, "I can attest to you not being like any female I've met.

"What do I tie you up with?" Bouncing with excitement over her small victory.

"I'll set up the straps. My safe word is oranges. That means you stop immediately," he warns as he lets her go gently so she won't fall backward.

"Why oranges?" She asks with a tilt of her head.

"Because I dislike oranges. I thought it was appropriate," he answers with a laugh.

"How can anyone dislike oranges?" She asks in disbelief with facial features to match.

"They give me hives," he answers with a shrug as he pulls something out of a drawer. Turning his focus on the object, he begins to attach them to his bed frame.

"Oh. Well, that's a good thing to know about you," she replies as she watches him finish up. Once he finishes, he begins to get undressed and she shamelessly watches. "You're so handsome," she adds with a smile.

"Thanks," he replies with a smile. "I don't think I've seen anyone come close to your beauty." She decides to snort as a reaction to his compliment. He walks over to her quickly and grabs her. Pulling her tightly to him and giving her a searing kiss. "Don't doubt my compliments ever again," he warns with irritation, "I don't have your wounds to cloud my judgment."

With that, Savannah simply nods. What can she say to that? He's right about that. From what he's told her about his upbringing, he was raised with love and understanding. A slight pang of jealousy hits her. She'll never be able to redo her childhood. Never know what it's like to grow up being loved unconditionally. Never know what it's like to have a parent she can go to whenever she has questions or issues with life. How different would her life have been if she grew up with that?

He clears his throat to interrupt her train of thought to ensure she pays attention to the instructions on how to bind his ankles and wrists. "Try to escape," she instructs after she ties all four. He does his best to break free and only manages one leg. After she fixes it, he tries again. This time, he's met without success. She then pulls a sleeping mask out of her purse and saunters over to him. "I've read that a blindfold will heighten your sensation."

"Savannah, no. I want to watch you," he tries to persuade.

She laughs. "I'm in charge and I say no." She begins to slowly take off her shirt. Revealing a little more skin with each movement. Once she reveals she wasn't wearing a bra, to begin with, she hears him suck in air through his teeth. Teasing with the waistband, she pulls them back up where they belong. Turning around, she begins to bend over as she pulls her pants down to reveal a bare ass.

"You've been commando this whole time? How did I not feel that?" He asks with disbelief.

"My sweatpants are thick enough. Where are the condoms?" She asks while scanning the room.

"In my duffle bag," he answers along with a jut of his chin.

Walking over to him she places the blindfold on. Giving him a minute to adjust, she goes into his bag and retrieves the box. "Last one." Walking to the side of the bed without making a noise, she begins to lightly rake her nails from his stomach to his chest. He flinches at contact and it makes her giggle. She leans in and gives him a tease of a kiss and he starts to groan once she pulls away. Slowly, she begins to kiss softly along his jawline, down his neck, and across his chest.

"Please take off the blindfold," he begs. This is pure torture.

"No," she says sternly.

She kisses her way down his chest, further down to his stomach, and drags her tongue across the sensitive spots of his hips. Blowing air on the fresh trail and sending chills. He sucks air in through his teeth. Without even the slightest hint of hesitation from her, she continues to kiss further down his body.

Sitting up straight, she begins to admire how well his cock stands at attention. Remembering how wonderful it feels to stand at attention inside of her. Leaning forward while grabbing ahold of his cock, she places a kiss on the tip of his head. The way the pooling bead of cum feels against her lips is so slippery and smooth. She always licks it off her lips to taste his delicious flavor.

"Savannah, this teasing is driving me crazy," he groans.

"Good," she says with a smile he cannot see, but hopes he can hear. Taking her tongue, she drags it along his shaft. Licking him up and down and adding air now and then.

"Savannah, this is torture," he grunts as he tries to yank his hand free from the restraints.

Without responding, she starts stroking his cock with her hands. Spitting on the tip to make the strokes nice and slippery. The sensation makes him groan loudly. Finally, she takes him inside her mouth to allow her hands the freedom it needs to rip open the condom. She can feel him try to thrust himself further into her mouth. Taking her mouth off of him, she smartly says, "impatient, much?"

"Savannah, ride me," he orders.

Grabbing his cock again she strokes it. "You're not in charge, I am. I'm enjoying this sense of control. I knew you wouldn't be fond of relinquishing the reins," she teases. Sliding the condom on with stealth, she gets into the reverse cowgirl position. This is a position she's had in her head for a few days now. He mentioned something about it in conversation, but she never asked to try it. It's not something she feels confident in doing while he can watch her. He would see her in all her awkward glory trying to figure out what she was doing. Lifting on her knees, she then lowers herself onto him.

"Savannah, I want to see," he demands. He can feel which position she's in and it's killing him to not watch.

Instead of answering him, she giggles. She begins to grind against him. Rocking back and forth at a slow pace. There's something about this position that feels better than cowgirl. The feeling of his balls against her clit creates suction and it makes the stimulation feel incredible.

He has had enough of the teasing. He's never been tied up before and he dislikes the inability to see and take control. Slowly, he begins to free one of his wrists from the binds. Since Savannah chose to face away from him, she wasn't able to see him rip the blindfold off. The sight of her from behind while grinding on him takes his breath away. Maybe it's because she thinks he can't see her, but she's finally riding him with such confidence. Slowly and carefully, he frees his other hand. There's no more willpower left in him to keep his hands off of her. He grabs her by the waist and rocks her harder. He really should let her have her fill, but he can't keep his hands off of her anymore.

"Thomas!" She gasps loudly. His hands scared her. She should've looked back to check on him. His silence should've been a red flag. With nothing left for her to do, she decides to hold onto him. He's rocking her so fast that she feels as if she might fall forward at any moment.

He can feel his arm burning from rocking her back and forth with such strength. Knowing she's almost at her peak is making him push past it. He can always tell by her breathing. There's just something about the change of rhythm that he's attuned to. He pushes and pulls her faster and faster until he feels her contract around him.

Taking advantage of her boneless state swaying off of him, he thrusts her to the side with his hips. Sitting up, he rips the binds off of his ankles and gets onto his knees. After folding her into the doggy-style position, he slams inside of her. Savannah gasps at the abrupt penetration. Slamming in and out of her with such speed. Her ass looks so amazing from this angle and he can't help but spank her. With determination to satisfy her twice, he continues to pump away. Grabbing ahold of her hair, he pulls to make her arch backward. Demanding, "play with your clit."

When he lets go of her hair, she does just that. Rubbing in circular motions to bring herself closer to another climax. Round and round her fingers go until it's all too much. "Thomas!" She screams out in pleasure as she explodes for the second time.

Feeling her the second time was his undoing. Groaning loudly as he finds his release. There's an endless amount and wonders if he could fill a bucket. After feeling empty, he decides it's time to pull out. Holding the condom at the base, he pulls himself out of her. "Oh, shit!"

A boneless Savannah barely manages to lift her head to look toward him, "what's wrong?"

"The condom broke inside of you," he says in a panic. How can he not panic? He filled her so much he can see it dripping out of her.

Chapter Twenty-Nine

"Savannah, take a walk with me to check the perimeter," Kate asks as she walks up behind Savannah and Thomas who's watching the calf they're raising. The calf doesn't need them as much now as it did when it first arrived. There's a mama cow who has sort of adopted it. She won't allow him to nurse, but she protects it from the other cows. Better than nothing.

"You really do need to walk heavier, you scared me!" Savannah says while holding her chest after she jumped. Thomas just turns around to look at Kate as if it's the most natural thing to have her sneak up on him. He might be used to it since he's worked with her for so long, but she isn't.

"But I enjoy being stealthy," Kate says with a huge grin. "Good morning, Thomas. Archer needs your help with the fence that separates the cattle from the goats."

"Good morning, Kate. I'll head over there now since the two of you are going for a walk," Thomas replies. After kissing Savannah on the top of her head, he begins to walk away.

"I'll return her after the walk," Kate shouts.

"Aunt Kate, we can be apart. It won't kill us," Savannah says with an eye roll.

Kate just laughs. "Come on, kid. Let's go stretch our legs."

It's been a relatively quiet morning for Savannah. She and Thomas woke up and went about their usual routine. Except, it wasn't too usual. They've both been unnaturally quiet. She didn't even question his silence. She's been too lost in her thoughts. She should be having thoughts of the condom breaking, but that's not even what she's worried about. She might not know a lot about reproduction, but she does know that it's hard to get pregnant when she's not regular with her cycle. She has her period 3-4 times a year. It's been like that since she started and she's never questioned it. She's been thankful for the infrequent cycle for the most part since it's always a painful mess.

It's the comment Kate made about him loving her. How does one even know when that happens? Is she so dysfunctional that she can't even decipher what loving someone is? Emotion was never a big thing in her household growing up. Her aunt showers her with affection. Savannah loves her family. Her feelings toward Thomas are not the same as the love she has for them. Is it supposed to feel different? "How does one know they're in love?" She asks abruptly.

"Um, okay…. How does that fit into what I was saying about the new pond project?" Kate asks with amusement.

"Oh, I didn't even realize you were talking to me. I guess I was lost in thought. I'm sorry," Savannah says with a tail between her legs. At least it would be if she had one.

"I'm just kidding. I was about to talk about that before you beat me to it with your question. I just wanted to see if you were paying attention," she says while laughing. Savannah deadpans. The look on her face makes her laugh even harder. "I'm sorry, kid. Let's get back to your question," Kate pauses to think about it. After a few moments, she says, "I would assume it's different for most people. Love for me means not being able to imagine myself without that person in my life. How happy the person makes me. How much I want my day to begin and end with them. Loving someone who isn't related to you, is different. When I first realized it with Noah, it terrified me. Not because love is scary in a bad way, but because I realized how much I wanted to let my guard down around him. I wanted him more than I wanted to breathe the air that fills my lungs. To be that vulnerable is a scary thing for me."

"I think I have some of those feelings for Thomas, but not quite the same," Savannah says with a quizzical look on her face.

"Again, it's not the same for everyone. I'm sure not everyone would agree with my description of it either. Can you envision a life with him? A life that extends beyond the next couple of years?" Kate asks with a smile.

"Yes. But I don't know if that's how he feels. I can't bring myself to ask what'll happen when summer is over. He'll go back to school and I'll be here at the farm," Savannah says with a little bit of sadness in her voice.

"Try having a nice dinner with him away from the control your hormones have over your body. A place you know you can't be led to distraction with intimacy," Kate answers. Hopefully, Savannah won't be able to tell how uncomfortable these conversations make her. She's always had an open-door policy with her kids and nieces. Even when the conversations bite her in the ass.

"That might work," Savannah says with a little bit of hope in her voice.

Instead of responding, Kate throws her arm around Savannah's shoulder and urges her to continue walking. They haven't made it very far. Past the cattle pasture and slightly past the newly planted trees that border Archer's little piece of earth. As they continue to walk along the tree line to check on the bison, she hears the snap of some twigs behind them. Not thinking much of it, she doesn't even bother to turn around. A few more yards and a voice she never wanted to hear again, sends chills down her spine.

"Looks like you're keeping yourself nice and fit, Kate," a man says loudly.

Whipping her head around, she spots him. "Why the fuck are you here? You're not allowed on my property," Kate says with anger as she fully turns around. He looks, worn. Being imprisoned was not kind to him. His hair is completely gray, his skin is leathered, his eyes are still brown with a cold emptiness, and he is bigger than he used to be. Sort of fit by the appearance of his arms, but his gut gives the impression that he's done a lot of sitting. His voice is the same as it's ever been. If she hadn't heard him first, she would've had to take a double take from his looks alone.

"I'm here to see my kids. Look at how you've grown, Hazel," the man says approvingly as he looks Savannah up and down.

While Savannah tries to hide behind her, Kate pipes up, "this is not Hazel. How could she possibly be this age? You haven't been gone that long. You need to go, Peter."

"Not without my kids," Peter says with irritation.

"You're not going anywhere with my children," Kate matches his irritation.

"Who is this?" Savannah asks with confusion.

"Oh, she's never mentioned me? Out of sight out of mind, Kate? Having me locked up in prison did a number on me. I lost a huge part of my life!" Peter begins to yell with anger.

"YOU? You lost a huge part of your life? Fuck you. You stole my security. You stole my ability to do a lot of things one would consider normal. You're lucky the only thing that happened to you was going to prison," Kate yells in return. "How did you even find me?"

"It wasn't hard. I had numerous years to do some digging while I was in prison. I've known where you were for years. Just got out a few months ago. Needed to take care of a few things before I paid you a little visit," Peter says smugly.

"Nice little setup you have here. I like walking around at night. It's immensely peaceful."

It was as if his words punched her in the stomach. He's been here? What if he had taken the kids? Now she feels sick. She's felt so safe when in reality she shouldn't have. "You need to leave, now," Kate seethes.

"Who's going to make me? You? That man I see you walking around with? I'd like to see him try," Peter laughs. "I've missed you, Kate. Well, not all of you, just the spot between your legs."

"Go jump off of a cliff," Kate bites back while she begins to pull out her phone.

"Oh, no you don't," Peter says while he reaches out and rips the phone from her hands. Throwing it to the ground, he looks at Savannah, "don't move." Kate tries to walk away and peter grabs her by the wrist. As she swings her fist, he grabs the other hand and spins her around to hold her against him. "You're stronger than before. But I've had years that were dedicated to working out. I'm still stronger," his words were suddenly interrupted by Savannah screaming for him to let her go. "This doesn't concern you, now shut up," he says to Savannah. "Let's have one more session of fun, Kate," he whispers into her ear. As he begins to choke her, she decides to kick him in the shins. Instead of loosening his grip, he throws her onto the floor and straddles her. Holding both of her hands above her head with one of his, he starts to choke her again.

Gasping for air, Kate cannot help but think that Savannah needs to run to safety. What will happen to Savannah once she's passed out?

Savannah screams, "let her go!" She then proceeds to knee him in the back and hit his head. He lets go of Kate momentarily to grab Savannah and throws her to the ground.

Kate watches in horror as Savannah's head lands harshly against the solid ground. "Savannah!" Kate screams. No response, not even a twitch. Kate begins to sob as she's being held on the ground

"Now, back to that session," Peter says with his hands around her neck once more, "I think I'll do it when you're blacked out. You won't be able to fight me then. Just like old times, right?" Kate tries her hardest to struggle while he's choking her. "Since she's not my daughter, I've decided to fuck her also. She can wake up naked next to your naked dead body."

Kate's eyes widen with alarm. No! Fighting as hard as she can against him even as she starts to see spots.

Satisfied that she's sufficiently out, he begins to rip open her flannel. Revealing her bra, he begins to work at her pants. A sudden hit against his head knocks him off of her.

Getting a cryptic text from Savannah was alarming. Especially since she was kidnapped not too long ago. "Trees. Help," was not much to go on, but he knew the general area to go look. Running past the trees, he scans the area. The sight of a man bent over a lifeless Kate and a lifeless Savannah nearby felt like a punch to his stomach. Once the man started to rip her clothes, he began to see red. Running up behind the man, he swings with full force. No time to check and see if they're alright, he needs to take care of this asshole. Without even stopping, Noah begins pounding away at the man. Who's going to stop and ask questions after what he just saw? After a few moments, the man begins to come back from being disoriented and begins to put up a fight. Each of them lands blows at the other while rolling on the ground trying to get better leverage.

A moan from Kate as she begins to stir distracts Noah. Peter gets the upper hand and knocks Noah over and straddles him to begin choking. Noah tries hitting his arm as best as possible, but there's nothing he can do against the downward force of Peter's strength. Glancing in the opposite direction, he sees a rock within arm's length. Quickly grabbing it, he swings and hits Peter in the face. A tear across his forehead with blood streaming out disorients him enough to loosen his grip. Noah takes advantage and knocks him off while landing one final blow with the rock still in his hand at Peter. Resting for just a moment on his back, he hears the gunshot, then feels the blood splatter across his face. Who's blood? He doesn't feel as if he's been shot.

Looking around frantically, he sees her. Kate, standing over the man's body with a gun in her hand. Getting to his feet as quickly as he can, he rushes over to her and wraps her in his arms. She's not speaking, not shaking, her eyes are blank, and her face is lacking emotion. Now's not the time to ask what's going through her head. After a brief moment, she bursts out of his arms to rush over to Savannah.

Thankfully, she's still breathing. Soft moans escape Savannah, but she cannot be roused. Sufficed that she's breathing, Kate walks back over to Noah who's near Peter's dead body. Wrapping her arms around Noah as he wraps his around her, she feels a kiss atop her head.

Once she came to, all she could focus on was stopping him. She watched in horror as Peter began straddling Noah. With a sense of purpose, she began looking around for anything to assist her husband in fighting for their lives. The sunlight reflecting against the metal body of a revolver caught her eye. Peter's gun. She recognized it from years back when she saw it on his mother's mantel. It belonged to his grandfather.

"Who was he?" Noah asks quietly.

"Their biological father," Kate responds while staring at the body.

"I think the rock would've sufficed," Noah tries to tease. Anything to get a semblance of a reaction from her. "Who does that gun belong to?"

"Him. I found it on the ground next to me. I had to do it. I had to know he will never haunt my dreams again," Kate says without emotion.

Chapter Thirty

The pop of a gunshot in the direction of Kate and Savannah is not what Thomas wanted to hear. There is no denying Archer heard it as well. The moment the sound rang from a distance, both of their heads turn in that same direction. Not even a full breath is taken before they begin to run toward the noise. No idea where the sound came from, just the knowledge that it was beyond the cattle pasture. Knowing that Kate hasn't carried a weapon on her since she shot Seth, terrifies him. Who is on the property with a gun? Who would've been shot? Rusty is in prison.

Ignoring the ache in his lungs from running, he keeps going. Archer is a surprisingly fast runner and he's keeping up with him without a complaint. As they pass the cattle pasture, his ears strain to hear any sort of sound. Nothing. Continuing to run past the trees, they see them. Kate holding Savannah, and Noah is on the phone near a man on the ground.

Rushing up to Savannah, whose eyes are closed, he asks Kate, "what happened?"

"She got thrown to the ground and she's yet to wake up," Kate says with concern. "Noah is on the phone with 911."

"Why is it always her? She doesn't deserve it," Thomas starts to break down next to Kate.

"Can you please hold her so I can see if Noah needs anything?" Kate doesn't need to help Noah or even want to let her niece go, but Thomas needs to hold her. He would never ask her to give Savannah over to him and he doesn't have to. The look of desperation on his face says it all for him.

He watches Kate get up and walk over to Noah and wrap her arms around him. Archer hasn't said a word the entire time. He's been looking at the body while standing next to it. Looking at the body with a look of anger Thomas has never seen on his face before. Archer can be serious when he needs to be, but never this serious. If the man weren't so obviously dead, Thomas thinks Archer would've finished him off. Who is that man?

With Savannah in his arms, he begins to run his fingers through her hair. Petting it in a way one would do to a loved one who is sleeping. He can feel a knot on the back of her head. He'd be willing to be that she has a concussion since she's asleep. "Please be okay," Thomas urges.

The moment he finishes his words, she begins to violently shake. "Kate!" Thomas yells once he realizes she is having a seizure. He places her down while also making sure there's nothing for her to hurt herself on. Eyes fully on her, he can hear Kate crying off to the side. There's nothing they can do until the ambulance gets there.

After a few minutes, she stops seizing. The paramedics show up not long after and haul Savannah and Thomas to the hospital. The police show up as they're loading her up and Kate already knows she can't go with them. She has to stay behind and explain why there's yet another dead body at her ranch.

The paramedics do what they need to do to control Savannah's vitals during the drive to the hospital. Thomas has his eyes glued to Savannah the entire time to make sure nothing gets worse. Also hoping that she miraculously wakes up from all of this. The ride feels like an eternity. Every minute is precious and he needs answers. He needs her.

Once at the hospital, they wheel her off for tests. This is all getting to be very familiar. Thomas has never wanted to be on this side of familiar at a hospital. He wants to be the one saving lives, not the one being utterly helpless. He's had a life of being in control and this is far from it. He's barely finished his first year of classes. They haven't even touched a subject that would've helped him in this scenario.

Elbows on his knees, head in his hands, and his mind racing with all the possible outcomes that he didn't even hear Kate and Noah sit next to him. A gentle hand starts rubbing his back and he looks up to find them. Not a single word is exchanged between the three of them as Thomas begins to cry along with Kate.

Two very anxious hours later…….

When the three of them are brought to the room Savannah is in, the doctor explains the TBI is the reason behind her seizures. That she started to have them again while they were running tests and the team gave her medication to stop them. They did everything they could and now they must wait to see what happens next. Seeing Noah consoling Kate who's crying uncontrollably, makes his heart ache to hold Savannah as such. The one person he wants comfort from is lying in the hospital bed. She's the only person who can put his heart at ease.

The nurses give the three of them pillows and blankets since neither of them is willing to leave until she has woken up. Archer is at the house with Hazel and Christian. Kate looks up briefly to thank the nurse. The only way she will be getting any sleep is if exhaustion forces her to do so.

"What did the police say?" Thomas asks as he's trying to distract himself.

"I told them everything. They have records of everything that happened before, so they know there are prior issues between us. I'm also advised not to leave the state," Kate says with an eye roll.

"Who was he?" Thomas finally asks. He's been waiting for the right time since he saw the man's body lying on the ground.

"Peter. Hazel and Christian's biological father," Kate replies without much emotion in her voice. "Let's focus our good thoughts on Savannah. You should get some sleep, Thomas. I'll take the first watch."

"I'm going to bring my chair next to her bed. We haven't slept apart since she returned and I don't think I'll be able to sleep if I'm not touching her skin," Thomas says while moving the chair closer to the bed.

"That's so cute. Just make sure you're not in their way when they come to check on her," Kate suggests.

Opening his eyes, he finds himself lying in the hospital bed next to Savannah. Kate and Noah are sleeping while sitting up in the chairs. First watch my ass. She fell asleep on the job. Looking over, he sees all the tubes Savannah is hooked up to. The wires flow all around the bed to monitor her progress. How can one person have such bad luck in life?

Thomas pulls out his phone to find something to entertain himself. If he's going to take this next watch, he needs something that will keep him awake.

Suddenly, the alarms on her machine start going off. He turns this way and that to see which machine is making the noise. When he reaches for the call button, the nurses already begin rushing into the room. "Get off the bed! We already told you not to lie next to her," one nurse says in anger. Thomas jumps out of the bed to allow the nurses to tend to Savannah. "Get the doctor!" Another nurse yells.

"What's going on?" Thomas demands loud enough to wake up Noah and Kate. The medical team either didn't hear him or they are ignoring him to focus on her. He's betting on ignoring him since he asked more loudly than he ought to have.

Kate begins to cry into Noah's chest as more nurses and doctors swarm into the room. None of this looks good. "No, this can't be happening!" Thomas says in anger.

The alarms on her machine continue to go off as they continue to work on her. "It's time to call it," one of the doctors says.

"What?" Thomas says with rage as he runs to the bed that Savannah's body is on. "No!" he cries.

"Thomas!" Kate says while nudging him.

"No!" He says as he jerks back toward Savannah.

"Thomas!" Kate persists as she begins to shake him.

"No, you can't take her from me!" Thomas demands. The feel of Noah pulling him backward tore at his heart. They can't take her away from him. He needs her. He loves her. Why is life so cruel? Giving him this amazing person just to rip her from him.

"Thomas!" Kate yells from a distance.

"Wake up, Thomas!" Noah demands.

The sound of Noah's voice makes him open his eyes. Once they're open, he notices the sound of the machine going off again. Terror fills his face. He's living the same scenario all over again.

"Thomas, move! You're messing with the oxygen monitor. The machine won't shut up until you get off of it," Kate says with irritation.

Taking a moment to absorb what was just said, he finally moves to allow the nurse to fix the monitor. "I thought she was dying," he finally speaks up.

"Aw, honey," Kate says with a motherly tone, "she's a fighter."

"She has to fight through this. I won't accept anything less," Thomas says with sadness in his voice and tears in his eyes.

"That's up to Savannah's body to decide. The doctors have done what they can and we need to wait and see if her body will pull through this," Kate replies sadly.

Chapter Thirty-One

Three days later……..

"Why won't her mom or dad show their face? It's been three days!" Thomas says with outrage. "Their daughter is lying in a hospital bed."

"We haven't seen her mom in years. I wouldn't know how to get ahold of her even if I wanted to. Don't count on Dylan showing up. He said lots of mean things when I told him what happened. He's an ass, to say the least. Savannah is better off without him," Kate answers as she tries to not get riled up again. The conversation she had with Dylan left her fuming. He had mentioned that after the ranch incident, they were both already dead to him. How someone can be so cold-hearted, she will never know. "He has taken this opportunity to drop the last of Savannah's things off at the ranch. Noah supervised the drop-off. I have to get back to my kids. I brought you some clean clothes and toiletries. Please let me know if anything changes."

"Thank you," Thomas replies. What more can he say? What more does he want to know? Anything else would just upset him further. What kind of a father won't put his stubbornness aside and visit his child in the hospital?

What he needs is a good night's sleep. Sleeping in a recliner is not his ideal bed. It's been killing him to not sleep in the same bed as Savannah. He hasn't tried again since he messed up her monitor. He's afraid he'll mess up something more important that will mess with her chances of pulling through. The nurses are thoughtful enough to arrange the monitors at night so he can place the chair to one side of her without being in the way of their job. His heart aches for her.

It's late and he better get some rest.

The next morning.......

"Why does my head hurt so bad?" Savannah says softly as she feels the tenderness of her head. Wincing once she reaches the particular spot she must have fallen on. Unlike the fraternity party, she remembers the events that happened with Kate and that guy. She remembers trying to help Kate and he knocked her off.

Opening her eyes, she finds herself in a hospital bed once more. This time, she has more things connected to her. Thomas is next to her in a chair and sleeping in the most uncomfortable-looking position. His facial hair has grown into more than stubble. How long has she been asleep? No one else is in the room. Why? "Thomas?" She calls softly. She's never seen his eyes fly open so fast. Carefully watching him watch her. What is he waiting for?

"Savannah," he whispers as tears start to flow down his cheek, "I've been so scared,"

"Why? What did I miss?" She asks softly with widening eyes.

"You almost died. You've been in a coma for three days and today would've been the fourth. The doctors weren't sure if you were even going to wake up," he says with tears continuing to stream down his cheeks.

"Hey, come here," she urges. Gently sitting on the bed, he pulls her into an embrace. Turning her lips to his ears, she whispers, "I love you."

He freezes. Pulling himself back to look into her eyes, he sees sincerity. He leans in to place a kiss on her lips. Softly at first, then the hunger he had for her is pouring out into their kiss. "Savannah," he says with a raspy voice, "marry me. I love you more than I can explain with words or actions. I want you to be the first thing I see in the morning and your lips to be the last thing I touch before I go to sleep. The thought of losing you shook me so hard. I've been such an idiot before. I should have told you the moment I realized it."

She looks at his handsome face and just smiles. This man. This silly man. He wants to be hers? Forever? Pulling him into a deep kiss, forgetting they're in a hospital room, she starts to lean back while pulling him along. During their descent, she breaks their kiss long enough to say, "yes!" As soon as her head hits the pillow, she also cries out, "ouch!"

He forgot where they were for a moment. Lost in the need to have her, he forgot her injuries. As soon as she cries out in pain, he jolts upward and pulls her up with him. "You have to be careful. You have a pretty nasty injury to your head. You even began to seize when I found you. Scared the shit out of me."

Her eyes widen at his words. "Looks like you'll forever be taking care of my wounds. You sure you want to marry me?"

"You're good practice for when I get into medical school," he teases in return. He pushes the nurse button to keep himself in check. All he wants to do is take her home and ravish her. There are lots of things he can do without her head touching a pillow.

During the time the doctors and nurses came in to check on Savannah, Thomas was able to call Kate and fill her in. Kate and Noah were already on the way to the hospital when they received the call, so they got there in no time at all with a large bouquet.

Once the medical staff leaves the room, Kate pipes up, "the flowers were the kid's idea. How are you feeling, Murphy?" Instead of words, Savannah returns with a scowl.

"Murphy?" Thomas pauses for a brief moment, "like Murphy's law?" Instead of answering, Kate just returns with the biggest grin he's ever seen.

"That's just rude!" Savannah retorts.

Kate, Noah, and Thomas just laugh.

Made in the USA
Middletown, DE
03 April 2023

27624894R00141